DIAL L FOR LOSER

A CLIQUE NOVEL BY LISI HARRISON

LITTLE, BROWN AND COMPANY

New York ⌁ Boston

If you like THE CLIQUE, you may also enjoy:

Bass Ackwards and Belly Up by Elizabeth Craft and Sarah Fain

Secrets of My Hollywood Life by Jen Calonita

Haters by Alisa Valdes-Rodriguez

Little, Brown and Company

Hachette Book Group USA
1271 Avenue of the Americas, New York, NY 10020
Visit our Web site at www.lb-teens.com

First Edition: August 2006

The characters and events portrayed in this book are fictitious. Any
similarity to real persons, living or dead, is coincidental and not intended
by the author.

ALLOYENTERTAINMENT   Produced by Alloy Entertainment
151 West 26th Street, New York, NY 10001

ISBN 978-0-316-11504-9

10 9 8 7 6 5 4
CWO
Printed in the United States of America

*To all the girls who've written me asking to star in the
Clique movie . . . this one is for you.*

CLIQUE novels by Lisi Harrison:

THE CLIQUE

BEST FRIENDS FOR NEVER

REVENGE OF THE WANNABES

INVASION OF THE BOY SNATCHERS

THE PRETTY COMMITTEE STRIKES BACK

DIAL L FOR LOSER

IT'S NOT EASY BEING MEAN

On their first school-free morning, the Pretty Committee gathered at Starbucks in the Westchester Mall and drank to their expulsion from Octavian Country Day.

"To Principal Burns and Mr. Myner." Massie Block lifted her low-fat sugar-free iced vanilla crème.

Claire Lyons folded her arms across her chest while Alicia Rivera, Dylan Marvil, and Kristen Gregory raised their white cardboard cups. It was her first winter away from Florida and she was still adjusting to the cold. Her lips were so chapped it looked like she had been making out with the zipper of her puffy blue jacket.

"Hello?" Alicia widened her brown eyes and glared at Claire's Chantico drinking chocolate, which was still on the table.

"Oops, sorry." Claire immediately scooped up the offending beverage and held it high.

Massie nodded in approval, then continued.

"To Principal Burns and Mr. Myner: Thank you for kicking us out of OCD." Her amber eyes flickered with delight. "From this day forward, stores are the new classrooms. Salespeople are the new teachers. Food courts are the new cafeterias. And Visas are the new seventh-grade ID cards."

1

"Ayyy-men!" Alicia hooted.

"Ayyy-men!" echoed the others.

"Jinx!" Claire giggled for the first time since she had been expelled.

The girls looked at one another, then snickered into their palms.

They were wearing what Claire and her best friend, Layne, secretly referred to as "black-tie sweats"—those velvety, two-hundred-dollar tracksuits that Massie described as "casual-cute." Claire, on the other hand, was "casual-casual" in a long-sleeved red tee and the nail-polish-stained Citizens of Humanity jeans she'd "borrowed" from OCD's lost-and-found before Christmas break.

"What?" Her heart started to race. "Don't you say 'jinx' here? Is it a Florida thing? I could teach it to you."

Massie knit her freshly waxed eyebrows. "Silly rabbit, *jinx* is for kids."

Everyone snickered again.

"Should we tell her?" Alicia asked.

Claire's cheeks warmed.

"Sure, whatevs." Massie shrugged.

"Jinx is so second grade," Alicia explained. "We're all about apple-C now."

"Oh, okay." Claire used her thanks-that-really-clears-things-up-for-me tone, hoping they could fast-forward to something that didn't make her feel like a foreign-exchange student.

Kristen sighed. "Apple-C is the keystroke on a Mac that—"

"I know." Claire suddenly got it. "It's the shortcut for *copy*, so you say it when someone is copying you." She would have finished with a *duh* but if *jinx* was second grade, *duh* was probably pre-K.

"Moving on." Massie jiggled the mountain of ice inside her plastic cup. "Here's to the Pretty Committee and the endless shopportunities that lie ahead."

"To the Pretty Committee and the endless shopportunities that lie ahead." The girls clinked, then drank.

"Apple-C!" Claire practically shot out of her seat.

"That was a toast, Kuh-laire." Massie rolled her eyes. "It doesn't count."

"Oh." Claire gulped her hot chocolate, accepting the burn on her tongue as punishment for being so stupid.

It had been six months since her family moved from Orlando to Westchester. Six months of living on the Blocks' estate, and six months of proving herself to the Pretty Committee. Finally, Claire was an official member, with an exclusive standing invitation to sleepovers, shopping trips, and five-way calls. But no matter how much fun the girls had together, she would wake up the next morning and need to impress them all over again. It was as if their leave-in conditioners seeped into their hair follicles while they slept and clogged their brains, permanently erasing "cool Claire" from their memories. There had to be *something* she could do to earn their full-time respect—but what? The more she tried to figure it out, the more elusive the answer became.

"We're living the American dream!" Dylan poked her finger though the creamy swirl on her caramel macchiato.

"Maybe *you* are," Kristen huffed. "But for *me*, this is a nightmare." She slammed her complimentary tap water on the table, ignoring the splash.

"I hear ya!" Claire gushed. "This place is so expensive they should call it Sixbucks. I'd much rather be in the OCD cafeteria. I'm over the Westchester."

"Ehmagawd!" Kristen recoiled. "Seriously?"

Claire stiffened, hating herself for saying the wrong thing—*again*. How could she have expected them to understand that at the mall she was just the new chick with a bad haircut, an empty wallet, and last year's jeans? But at school she was the mysterious outsider who, against all odds, had been accepted into the Pretty Committee. And that made her special.

"That was a joke, right?" Massie looked deep into Claire's eyes, silently urging her to take it all back. "You don't really want to be back at OCD, do you?"

"Of course not." She forced a huge smile. "This . . ." She opened her arms and turned to face the mall. " . . . is a total fantasy!" Claire silently thanked her parents for giving her three years of community theater acting lessons.

"I would *love* to share said fantasy." Kristen sighed. "But I have to do *this*." Her biceps twitched as she lifted the black Prada messenger bag the girls had bought her for her twelfth birthday. She turned it upside down and an avalanche of textbooks tumbled out. *A History of Western Philosophy, Philosophy Made Simple, Philosophy for Dummies,* and *The Oxford Dictionary of Philosophy* were among the titles.

Everyone stared.

"My mom is forcing me to study philosophy until I'm back at school," Kristen explained. "She wants me to figure out the meaning of life so I'll know exactly what I'm throwing away." Her blue eyes began to fill with tears. "Her words, not mine."

"She's probably mad because you lied." Alicia lifted a steaming cup of Sumatra to her glossy, light pink mouth.

Kristen sniffled. "What was I supposed to do? Miss out on our first boy-girl field trip because my parents couldn't afford it? Puh-lease!"

"You told them you were going away with your soccer team, then hopped a bus to Lake Placid." Alicia pinched off a piece of her low-fat blueberry muffin. "And while you were there, you got expelled *and* lost your scholarship."

"Yeah, I saw that episode," Kristen hissed. "No need for the recap."

Massie put an arm around her and gave her a loving squeeze. "I thought it was very brave."

"Me too." Alicia grinned.

"Same," Dylan added.

Kristen tugged a chunk of her short blond hair. "Why does it seem like I'm the only one who got punished?"

"Because you are," Dylan smirked. "My mom *can't* be mad at me. This whole thing is her fault. If she hadn't been hooking up with Mr. Myner in Lake Placid, I never would have run away. You guys never would have chased after me, we never would have gotten lost in the woods, and we'd be napping in science lab right now."

"Well, *I* got punished." Claire slouched. "My dad woke me up at six thirty a.m. this morning and made me shower and get dressed, like I was going to school."

The girls made pouty frowns to show how sorry they felt about Claire having been denied her beauty rest.

"Then," she continued, "at exactly seven thirty I had to go out in the cold and stand by the Range Rover for five minutes and act like I was waiting for Isaac to carpool me."

"Seriously?" Dylan's green eyes were wide with disbelief.

"Yup. And the worst part was . . ." Claire pointed to Massie. ". . . *your* bedroom light was still off."

Massie accepted a congratulatory round of high fives.

"That's not all." Claire leaned forward. "My dad asked Layne to e-mail me our homework. I have to do it all. Every night! And that's the only time I can use my computer. Which, by the way, he moved into the kitchen."

Everyone gasped.

"But the worst part is, I can't ride my bike to Cam's, and I haven't seen him since Lake Placid." She paused to count on her fingers. "That was five days ago!"

"He's a guy." Alicia tossed her long black hair. "Make him come to you. It's less pathetic."

Claire ignored the jab. "He's not allowed. No visitors until I'm back in school. Not even Layne."

"Well, I can do whatever I want," Massie smirked. "As long as I prove it's educational."

"How is shopping *educational*?" Kristen asked.

"Figuring out my change is math. And speaking to you is English."

Kristen rolled her eyes.

"If the school board doesn't let us back in, my dad's gonna sue," Alicia announced.

"When are they meeting?" Claire asked eagerly.

"April second."

"They better change their minds." Kristen ripped her crumpled napkin. "Or I'm getting homeschooled."

"I don't care if we don't go back." Massie glossed her lips with Baby Aspirin—the latest delivery from Glossip Girl. "I want to try boarding school in Switzerland."

"Me too." Alicia nodded.

"Ehmagawd, same!" Dylan sounded utterly shocked by the coincidence.

"Well, I'll be going to Abner Doubleday Day," Claire moaned.

"*Ew!*" Alicia gasped. "Public school?"

Claire nodded slowly.

Alicia checked over her shoulder, leaned forward, and whispered, "ADD is full of juvenile delinquents who steal your lunch, then force you to buy it back for a hundred dollars."

The thought of fighting her way to the top—again—made Claire shudder twice.

"They hate private-school girls there. They think we're spoiled."

"What do they know?" Dylan pushed back her cuticles with the corner of her American Express gold card.

"Zzzzzzzz," Massie fake-snored. "Can we puh-lease go shopping now?"

"Given!" Alicia clapped.

"I'll be here studying." Kristen moped. "I'm getting quizzed tonight on Socrates."

"We'll pick you up on our way out." Massie reached into her burgundy leather wallet, pulled out a twenty-dollar bill, and tossed it on the table. "For me, the meaning of life is a Frappuccino and a cinnamon biscotti. Study *that*."

"Thanks!" Kristen beamed.

The girls pushed back from the table and threw their bags over their shoulders. Claire waved goodbye to Kristen, then followed Massie, Alicia, and Dylan into the bright atrium.

"Let's go to Juicy," Dylan suggested.

"No," Alicia whined. "Neiman's."

"Let's start at BCBG and we'll work our way left," Massie insisted. "Don't worry, we won't miss a single store."

Claire stuffed her hands in her empty pockets and yawned. Her parents didn't need to ground her for getting expelled. Being sentenced to a lifetime at the mall was punishment enough.

Massie pulled a worn copy of *Us Weekly* from her leather Miu Miu shoulder bag and flipped to the red-carpet shot of Abby Boyd. The actress's dark boob-length mane was one part wave and two parts shine. It was a total ten.

"Isaac?" She unclipped her seat belt and tossed the magazine onto the driver's lap. "Does my hair look like *hers*?" Massie stroked her new hair extensions the same loving way she petted her devoted pug, Bean.

"Buckle up," he insisted, never taking his eyes off the road. Once they came to a complete stop, he lifted the glossy photo to his face. "Yours looks *better*." The corners of his eyes crinkled when he smiled. "I said that when I picked you up from the salon."

"Yeah, but that was five minutes ago—you could have changed your mind." Massie giggled so he'd think she was joking, even though she wasn't.

"Well, I haven't."

"Swear?" Massie held out her pinky.

"Swear." Isaac wrapped his baby finger around hers and shook. "You look like a glamorous movie star."

Massie leaned back in the cushy seat and winked at the picture of her favorite actress-slash-hair-muse. They were both wearing black tights, dark denim minis, and ankle boots. The only difference was their tops: Abby had on a white mesh see-through beater over a turquoise bra, while Massie had opted for a green-and-brown striped Ella Moss sweater. She had to draw the line somewhere.

"Where to?"

"Alicia's," Massie chirped. "The girls are waiting for me. We're going to the mall."

"Again?"

"Yup." She tried to sound excited, but after yesterday's six-hour spree it was clear that March was all about discounts on size-ten winter boots and XXL turtlenecks in primary colors. If only they had been expelled in December, during the holiday and resort collections, or in April, when the spring lines were out. But no—she was trapped in shopping limbo doomed to four weeks of sale-surfing. First school, now this—her entire life was on hold.

Isaac stopped in front of the iron gates that surrounded the Rivera estate and tapped the horn. It was impossible to see if the girls were coming, because a cluster of maple trees—which had somehow managed to keep their leaves through winter—blocked the stately stone mansion. But the familiar click-clack of heels assured Massie that her friends were only a few feet away. Quickly, she glossed her lips and smoothed her six-hundred-dollar 'do.

"Who's ready for another day at the mall?" she bellowed as the girls piled into the Range Rover.

"Shhhhh." Kristen pressed a finger against her mouth. "I'm supposed to be at the library."

"And I'm supposed to be at Alicia's, talking to her dad about the lawsuit," Claire whispered.

"I'm allowed to go to the mall." Dylan forced a camouflage cap over her thick red curls. "As long as I buy my mom a jar of La Mer face cream."

"I can do whatever." Massie gathered her extensions into a ponytail, then let them fall over her thin shoulders.

"Ehmagawd! Your hair!" Alicia squealed. "I totally heart it!"

"Huh?" Massie acted confused, like she had forgotten about it. Her beauty had to seem effortless, or they wouldn't be as awestruck. "Oh, you mean my extensions? You like 'em?"

"You look ah-mazing." Dylan tugged on her navy Daryl K scoop-neck sweater until it hung off her shoulder.

"Kind of like Abby Boyd," Kristen offered.

"I totally agree." Claire smacked her thigh.

"Really? Abby Boyd?" Massie tried to suppress the resounding *yay!* building inside her. "I never would have thought that." She stuffed the *Us Weekly* toward the bottom of her bag while avoiding Isaac's knowing glance in the rearview mirror.

"So, I was thinking." Kristen unbuttoned her lime-green coat and tossed her book-filled Prada in the very back. "Maybe instead of shopping . . . we should see a half-price matinee."

"Ew!" Dylan winced. "Those things are filled with old ladies who smell like pee and vitamins."

"Let's get our nails done." Alicia wiggled her fingers in the air.

Claire sighed. "It's too bad we aren't allowed on OCD property."

"Why?" Massie pinched her eyelashes to make sure her mascara hadn't clumped.

"Because Layne is leading a protest to get us back in. And it would be cool to watch."

"Hmmmm, Layne." Dylan twirled a red ringlet around her index finger. "I forget. Do we like her?"

"I do," Claire snapped, and turned to the window.

"What time is it happening?" Kristen asked.

"After school."

Massie consulted her Coach watch. "Isaac." She unbuckled her seat belt and put her hand on his shoulder. "Can you drop us on the corner of Birch and Worth?"

"I'm not taking you anywhere unless you buckle up."

She rolled her eyes. After nine years, Isaac was more like a second dad than the family driver.

"Here! This is perfect!" she shouted when he pulled up to the crosswalk. "We'll get out here."

"I'll pick you up in a half hour," Isaac announced. "Don't be late."

Kristen grabbed her Prada bag out of the backseat. "Ugh," she grunted as she hooked it over her shoulder. "These books weigh a ton."

Massie buttoned her white faux-fur jacket and put on her aviators, despite the gray sky. "Leave 'em in the car."

"Can't." Kristen sighed. "My mom is all-knowing."

"Does she know you're paranoid?" Massie slammed the door and Isaac drove off.

"Well, what if we get caught?" She adjusted her bag again.

"Big deal." Massie finger-combed the ends of her extensions. "It's not like they can expel us."

"Point." Alicia lifted her finger and drew an invisible number one in the air.

"They could cancel the board meeting and decide not to let us back in." Claire wrapped a multicolored polka-dot scarf around her neck.

"Lose the scarf and we won't get caught." Dylan giggled. "You can see that thing from space."

Everyone laughed.

"Let's go." Massie led the way toward campus. The faster she walked, the more her hair bounced and swayed. She felt free! No more homework, tests, or sweaty phys-ed classes. If she wanted to read magazines for five hours while Jakkob glued hair to her scalp, she could. Life was hers for the taking. So why did she feel like an empty tube of lip gloss, a hollow shell with nothing left to give?

"We should take cover in the faculty parking lot," Kristen suggested. "It gives us a perfect view of the Great Lawn and we can hide behind the cars."

"Fine, but we enter from the back," Massie added. "Hurry! The bell is going to ring in—"

"Fifty-five seconds," Kristen interrupted.

"Fifty-four seconds," Massie insisted. "Come awn!"

They scurried around the block giggling and shushing one another.

"Wait up," Alicia called. "You know I can't run."

"Just watch what we're doing and copy!" Dylan shouted.

"Apple-C!" Claire yelled.

"Not funny," Alicia panted.

They didn't stop until they reached the foot of the parking lot. "This is weird," Kristen whispered under her breath.

No one else said a word.

They stood gazing at the assortment of fuel-efficient cars that stood between them and their old school. Massie felt like a ghost of her former self, coming back from the dead to take a final glimpse at the life she was leaving behind . . . the life she had taken for granted.

She wanted to ask her friends if they missed the eraser smell of the halls. Or the rambling, dorky stories their English teacher would tell them about his hairless cats. Or text-messaging during study period or laughing during lunch or counting the compliments they'd get from the LBRs (losers beyond repair) or going to the soccer games at Briarwood Academy and flirting with their crushes. But she didn't. It was her job as the alpha to keep their spirits up. *They needed her.*

Rrrriiiinnnng!

"There it is," Massie announced. "It's showtime."

"Quick!" Kristen cried. "Get behind that VW."

"Which one?" Dylan panicked. "There are, like, ten of them here."

"The dirty white one with the 'Less Bombs, More Art Supplies' sticker." Kristen pointed to a beat-up car sandwiched between a GMC Jimmy and a gold Ford Taurus. "It's in the first row."

They crouched next to the expanding oil stain between the rear tires.

"Perfect view." Massie wiped her cold, clammy hands on her black tights. That same nervous flutter she'd felt in her stomach right before she lip-kissed Derrington in Lake Placid was back.

"Aren't you so glad we're free?" Dylan asked.

"Given," Alicia purred. "We can do whatever we want whenever we want. We don't *have* to come here ever again."

"It's true," Dylan agreed. "We're here because we *want* to be. Not because we *have* to be."

"Totally."

All of a sudden, a rush of girls burst through the doors. Most of them wore skinny jeans tucked into their knee-high boots, or Uggs with miniskirts. Some were laughing, while others were on their cell phones. Everything was exactly as it had always been. Even though Massie wasn't there.

"Kuh-laire," Massie hissed. "Where is this protest?"

Claire bit down on her thumbnail and shrugged.

Hahhhhh . . . Hahhhhh. The sudden roar of a cheering crowd interrupted.

"K, you're ringing," Massie snapped.

"Oops. Sorry." Kristen pulled a scratched silver phone out of her argyle sock and flipped it open. "Hi, Ma." She rolled her eyes. "Yes, I'm studying."

The girls giggled.

"What do you mean, prove it? How can I prove it?" Kristen opened and closed the Velcro strap on her green-and-white leather Pumas as she listened to her mother's instructions. "Are you serious? . . . Fine. No problem." She quickly flipped her messenger bag upside down and dumped the books on the asphalt.

"What is it?" Massie whispered. "What does she want?"

"Outta the way!" Kristen mouthed. "Hurry!"

They all jumped back, searching one another's faces for an explanation. When the area was clear, Kristen lifted her phone and snapped a picture of the pavement. She immediately forwarded it to her mother.

"Did ya get it?" She silently invited the girls back. "See, I told you I was alone. . . . Yes, I'm outside. I needed some air. The heat was blasting in the library and—" She paused. "Yes, I'll be home by five. Love you too." She stuffed her phone back in her sock and exhaled. "This protest better work. I can't handle this much longer."

"There she is!" Claire stabbed the air with her finger.

Layne was waving a sign made of white poster board that had been taped to a long twig. A grainy, blown-up shot of Claire smiling sweetly was taped to the front, and SAVE THE LYONS was painted across the back in big maroon letters. Two Gwen Stefani–wannabes with identical signs followed closely behind her.

"You know, if she would just brush her hair, get a few blond highlights to offset the mousiness, and stop shopping in the men's department of the Salvation Army, she'd have cute-potential," Dylan said. "She has nice blue eyes. Small, but nice."

"They're green," Claire murmured.

"Save the Lyons!" shouted Layne and her BFFs, Meena and Heather, as they poked the sky with their signs.

"Ehmagawd," Alicia screeched. "*This* is the protest?"

"I assumed it would be for all of us." Claire's cheeks turned bright red. "I am so sor—"

"Puh-lease! I'm glad Layne's not fighting for me," Massie said to the oil stain beneath her feet. "The last thing I need is for people to think we're friends."

"Point," Alicia uttered.

"This whole protest thing is stupid. I feel bad for you, Claire."

"Huh?" Claire tugged on her short honey-blond bangs. "Why?"

"I just think it may ruin your chances of getting back in." Massie checked her nails for dirt. "The board may think you're causing more trouble. They could see you as a threat."

"Really?" Claire's blue eyes were wide with fear.

"Yeah, but don't worry. We've taught you a lot. I'm sure you'll be fine at ADD."

Claire sat back on the frozen ground, hugged her knees to her chest, and lowered her head.

"Let's get out of here." Massie jumped to her feet. There was no way she was going to stick around to watch Claire's pathetic little fan club treat *her* like last year's Sevens.

"Wait!" Kristen grabbed Massie's ankle. "Look!"

A circle of at least thirty girls was forming in front of Principal Burns's office window with bigger, flashier, more fabulous signs than Layne's.

"Take pity on the Pretty Committee! Take pity on the Pretty Committee! Take pity on the Pretty Committee!" they chanted.

"Ehmagawd!" Massie crouched back down. "They're wearing purple tulips in their hair. My favorite color."

"Look." Dylan pointed. "That sign says, 'We Want Massie Back in Class-y.'"

"Love that!" Massie tapped her heart.

"I see one that says, 'Unblock the Block!'" Kristen chimed in.

"Ah-dorable!"

"Aren't you afraid you won't get back into school now?" Claire smirked.

Massie checked her reflection in a hubcap, ignoring Claire's jab.

"Ehmagawd, there's one for me!" Alicia clapped.

"Where?" Massie hissed.

"There." She pointed to Olivia Ryan, whose sign, ALISHA WE MISH-YA, doubled as an advertisement for her stupidity.

"Um, she spelled your name wrong." Kristen cackled.

"*So?*" Alicia glowered.

"Ehmagawd, Massie, look!" Dylan gasped.

Massie held her palm in front of Dylan's face, ordering her to wait. She was in the middle of counting and didn't want to lose her place. There was one sign for Alicia, three for Claire, and eighteen for her. Not bad. Of course, she'd be sure to tell her crush, Derrington, she'd had an even twenty-five.

"This is terrible," Dylan whined.

"The worst!" Kristen agreed.

"Don't be so sensitive." Massie put her arms around her friends. "Just because no one made signs with *your* names on them doesn't mean—"

"No!" Dylan barked. "Look! By the bike racks."

Massie steadied herself on the dust-covered VW.

Strawberry and Kori, Alicia's ex-friends from dance class, hopped on their Bratz bikes and tore across the lawn. They pedaled like Lance Armstrong and rang their rusty bells, shouting, "Out with the old, in with Da Crew!"

"Who do they think they are?" Massie cried. "Do they seriously think *they* can start their own Pretty Committee?"

"Don't they have to be *pretty* to do that?" Dylan scoffed.

"Are they really going to call it 'Da Crew'?" Kristen winced.

"Looks like they have some competition," said Claire.

Four petite blondes in matching yellow tennis dresses

charged across the lawn waving flags that said THE COUNTRY CLUB tied to vintage wooden rackets.

"What makes them think we're not coming back?" Massie shouted, forgetting they were on a stakeout.

Alicia stomped her foot. "My dad is so suing them."

"Why isn't Principal Burns breaking this up?" Massie searched the lawn. There wasn't a single security guard out there.

"Doesn't OCD encourage freedom of expression and the right to protest?" Claire asked.

Everyone stared.

"She's right." Kristen sighed. "It's in the handbook. After we got expelled I read it cover-to-cover looking for a loophole."

"Great," Massie said to the tangled charm bracelet around her wrist. The thought of being replaced by Da Crew or the Country Club—after her lifelong struggle to become number one—made her quake. So what if eighteen girls wanted her back? Six didn't, and if she didn't do something soon—something to remind them how insanely fabulous she was—there would be more.

CURRENT STATE OF THE UNION

IN	OUT
Gluing my hair	Growing my hair
Hanging at the malls	Hanging in the halls
Da Crew & the Country Club	The Pretty Committee!!!!!

Claire knelt on the sea-green tiles inside the Blocks' hot tub, trying her hardest not to disturb Massie or Massie's mother, Kendra, who had their backs pressed up against the bubbling jets and their eyes closed.

They were in the "wet section" of the elegant horse-shed-turned-spa: a marble oasis complete with steam room, sauna, and a walk-in-closet-size shower that had nozzles on every wall, so turning was an option, not a necessity. Tranquil New Age music played on a constant loop, and the calming smell of lavender soothed the senses. It used to be Claire's favorite place to unwind after a long day of studying. But these days it was merely an inexpensive way to pass the time.

"Mom, how do you do it?" Massie exhaled slowly, her eyes still closed.

"Do what, dear?" Kendra gathered her shiny brown bob into a tiny ponytail and lowered her head. A string of medium-size black pearls was all she had on, while Claire and Massie opted for the red one-pieces they used to wear in swim class at OCD.

"Nothing."

"Tell me, dear." Kendra turned to face her daughter.

"I mean *nothing*." Massie stomped her foot. "How do you do *nothing* all day? It's so hard."

Kendra rolled her thin neck from side to side. "Practice."

Massie's back stiffened. "Kuh-laire, don't go telling everyone I said that."

"I won't." Claire dunked her head and let out an underwater, "Yesss!" It was the first time Massie had admitted life without OCD was boring. Claire wasn't the only school-loving freak after all.

Massie splashed her when she resurfaced. "Why are you smiling?"

"I'm not." She grinned. But the truth was, being alone with Massie filled Claire with pure happiness. The instant the other girls left, it was like a director had yelled, "Cut!" They could stop acting cool and go back to being themselves: friends.

"Stop it!" a squeaky voice suddenly shouted. "No, don't! Don't! I'm serious!"

Kendra yanked her robe into the water, struggling to cover herself with a half-floating, half-sinking mass of white terry cloth. "Who's there?"

"Oof!" Tiny Nathan, Todd Lyons's pint-size partner in crime, practically flew through the beveled-glass door. "S-sorry." He steadied himself. "Someone pushed me." He giggled.

"Todd!" Massie and Claire shouted at the same time.

"Apple-C!" Claire whacked Massie's bare arm.

"Nice one." Massie chuckled.

"Thanks."

"Todd." Kendra inhaled, like she was gathering the strength to explain something complicated to him. "You boys need to get out of here. It's girls only right now."

His snicker was muffled by the gurgling jets.

"Todd!" Claire shouted.

"What? I didn't do anything," insisted the ten-year-old redhead.

"Did too!" Tiny Nathan's narrow brown eyes were fixed on Kendra's bare shoulders.

"Todd!"

"Okay, okay." Todd stepped into the steamy room and grabbed Nathan's frail arm. His entire face and body were covered in temporary tattoos—hearts, moons, dice, devils, barnyard animals, and busty fifties-style pinup girls. It looked like he had fallen asleep on an open comic book and rolled over twice.

"Ignore it," Claire muttered to Massie and Kendra. They quickly turned away to avoid laughing.

"Let's go." Todd tugged Tiny Nathan's X-Men sweatshirt. "They're boring."

"Yeah," Nathan squeaked.

The second they were gone, Kendra hoisted her soaked robe out of the tub and slapped the sopping heap of terry cloth onto the marble floor. "Ahhhhhhh." She let out a cleansing sigh and closed her eyes.

"Nice butts!" the boys shouted from the doorway.

"Todd!" Claire smacked the bubbling water.

The boys burst out laughing as they scurried outside.

"Did he lose a bet?" Massie asked, referring to Todd's body art.

"He's trying to get expelled from Briarwood." Claire crossed her eyes for a second. "He thinks we have it made right now."

"Oh, your poor mother." Kendra tapped her heart.

Massie touched the back of her head, checking the pins that held her extensions out of the chlorinated water. "Did he get in trouble?"

"Nope." Claire grinned. "Headmaster Adams is making him wear them to the St. Patrick's Day dance as his punishment."

"No way . . ." Massie's voice trailed off. "Funny."

Claire lowered her head and examined her pruning fingertips. "It's so stupid."

"What?" Massie rolled onto her stomach and kicked. "That we're banned from Briarwood?"

"Yeah." Claire nodded, loving when their minds were in sync.

"It makes sense to me." Kendra hooked a finger around her pearls. "Briarwood is OCD's brother school."

"Well, it's still stupid," Massie insisted.

"Do you think Cam and Derrington will go to the St. Patrick's Day dance without us?" Claire bit down on her already mangled thumbnail.

"I have to get out. I think I have heatstroke." Massie stood up slowly and wrapped herself in a fluffy yellow towel.

Ever since she and Derrington had lip-kissed in Lake Placid, she refused to talk about him. Was it because she didn't like him anymore, or because she was afraid he didn't like her? Claire was about to ask when Massie's ringing phone, which sounded exactly like Bean's bark, interrupted.

Yap-yap-yap . . .

Yap-yap-yap . . .

Massie reached for her purple-crystal-covered Motorola and flipped it open. "Hello? Yeah, I'll hold."

"Who is it?" Claire mouthed, praying it was Derrington. Because if it was, there was a good chance Cam would be with him. She fluffed her embarrassingly short bangs to make sure they hadn't split into an upside-down V.

"It's Dylan." Massie sighed.

An electronic voice came from Claire's cell. *Pick up the phone. . . . Pick up the phone. . . .*

Now *she* was ringing. Claire raised her hand out of the hot tub and patted the marble floor until she found her scratched Nokia.

Pick up the phone. . . . Pick—

"Hello?"

"Claire, it's Dylan."

"Hey."

"Massie, Alicia, Kristen, are you all on?" Dylan asked.

"Yup," they said at slightly different times.

"Gawd, these five-way calls are complicated." Dylan chomped down on what sounded like a handful of broken glass.

"Ew, what is that?" Massie stuck out her tongue like it was covered in dog food.

Claire covered her cell phone so the others wouldn't hear her giggling.

"Sorry." Dylan chewed. "I just ate a handful of bran flakes. I started my bran-only diet today."

A mischievous smile formed across Massie's face. "Do you want to borrow my knife?"

"Huh?" Dylan swallowed. "Why?"

"To help you cut the cheese!"

While everyone laughed, Massie opened the sliding glass door and entered the "dry section": a log-cabin-inspired meditation room with a roaring fireplace, sheepskin rugs, and wide leather club chairs draped in Ralph Lauren Navajo-style blankets.

Claire felt weird staying in the hot tub alone with naked Kendra, whose eyes were luckily still closed, and quickly hurried to join Massie.

"Are you sitting down?" Dylan asked.

"Yeah," they answered.

"Hold on." Alicia sounded out of breath. "Hold on. . . . Hold on. . . . Keep holding. . . . Okay. Sitting."

"Is everyone sitting *now*?"

"*Yes!*"

"Cool, because you are going to pass out eleven times when you hear this." Dylan was milking her good news like a Starbucks barista.

"*What?*" everyone shouted.

"Guess who is going to be on my mom's show this

Monday." Dylan sounded like she was jogging. "Take a wild guess."

"Lohan?"

"No."

"Simpson?"

"No."

"Bloom?"

"No."

"Hartnett?"

"No."

"Beyoncé?"

"No."

"Spears?"

"No."

"Maddox?" .

"No."

"Zahara?"

"*No!*" Dylan cracked up.

"Who?" Alicia whined.

"Keep guessing."

But it wasn't that easy. Merri-Lee Marvil was the host of *The Daily Grind*, the highest-rated morning show in the country. She could have anyone, from the biggest A-list celebrity in Hollywood to a tabby cat that knit scarves for the homeless.

"Come awn." Massie paced across the sheepskin rug. "It'll take us all day to figure it out."

"We've got nothing but time," Kristen groaned, clearly over the whole expelled thing too.

"Fine, I'll tell you." Dylan chomped down on another handful of bran flakes. "Ready?"

"Yes!" they all shouted.

"Apple-C!" they shouted again.

"Do you want to hear or not?"

"Ehmagawd," Massie giggle-yelled. "Tell us already."

"AbbyBoydandHadleyDurk!"

"What?" Claire asked. She could have sworn Dylan said, "Abby Boyd and Hadley Durk." But everyone knew that was impossible. They *hated* each other.

"Abby Boyd and Hadley Durk will be on *The Daily Grind* to talk about their new movie, *Dial L for Loser*."

Massie looked at Claire and screamed.

"What is it?" Kendra scrambled into the living room holding a yellow towel in front of her dripping body. "What happened? Is everyone okay?" Woozy from a sudden head rush, she grabbed the black granite mantle to steady herself.

"They never do interviews together." Massie jumped on the leather club chair and started bouncing. "How did—"

"Wait, that's not the best part," Dylan interrupted.

"It gets better?" Alicia squealed.

"Yup." Dylan sounded pleased with herself. She obviously liked being the one with all the information. "I have passes! We'regoingtomeetthem!"

"*Ahhhhhhhhhhhhh!*" Massie screamed.

"Me too?" Claire asked.

"Do you still live in Massie's guesthouse?" Dylan sounded like a nursery-school teacher.

"Uh-huh." Claire avoided Massie's amber eyes just in case the answer was—

"Then of course you too."

"*Ahhhhhhhhhhh!*" Massie and Claire screamed.

Kendra clutched her heart. "Hang up those phones right now before you give me a coronary."

Claire immediately hit end.

"Call ya later." Massie snapped her phone shut without question. She had been trying to stay on her mother's good side ever since they got expelled, to avoid punishment. And, like all of her ploys, it was working.

"What's going on?" Kendra poured a tall glass of cucumber water and sat on the arm of her daughter's chair.

"Mom, you don't understand. Abby Boyd and Hadley Durk are, like, the biggest teen celebrities in Hollywood. They're in every magazine on the planet." Massie paused, eyed Claire, and screamed. Claire screamed back, then they hugged.

Kendra fanned her cheeks with a copy of *Architectural Digest*. "What am I missing?"

"Abby and Hadley have been in a massive feud for over a year because Hadley thinks Abby hooked up with her boyfriend—correction, *ex*-boyfriend—the ah-dorable Palmer Dryden. This is their first interview together, ever! And we're going!" Massie turned to Claire and shrieked. The two girls hugged again, as if hearing the news for the first time.

"I'm not sure." Kendra shook her head. "You've been expelled. And this seems like a fun little outing to me."

"What?" Massie jumped to her feet. "No way! You can't."

Claire's heart pounded in protest.

"And exactly how is going to see your favorite movie star ed-u-cational?" Kendra raised her eyebrows and glared at her daughter.

Massie fixed on her mother's hazel eyes. "I'm gonna learn how a *live* TV show is made."

"Hmmm." Kendra tapped her chin while she contemplated this.

"And I'll be exposed to a bunch of new jobs I never knew existed."

"Hmmmm."

"And . . ." Her eyes were shifting as she searched for an answer. "And—"

"And she won't be spending any money at the mall," Claire jumped in.

Massie exhaled.

"Will you write Merri-Lee a thank-you note as soon as you get back?"

"Of course." Massie smiled sweetly.

"Claire, will one of the parents be there to supervise?"

"Uh—"

"Ahb-viously Dylan's mom will be there."

"Okay, then, I'm off to moisturize before Fendi commissions my dry skin for their fall handbag collection." Kendra tossed her magazine on the oak coffee table and padded back to the "wet section."

Claire's eyelids fluttered with excitement. "Wait until Cam and Derrington hear about this. They'll freak!"

"We *have* to let the girls at school know too." Massie tightened the yellow towel around her waist. "Da Crew and the Country Club will be so 'out' when everyone hears this."

"Let's call the boys and tell them." Claire held up her red Nokia. It had been exactly seven sleeps since she'd seen Cam Fisher and she didn't know how much longer she'd last. Ever since they'd lip-kissed on the Lake Placid trip, her crush had turned into full-blown love. She knew he felt it too. The proof was in the last C-note (as Cam so cleverly liked to call the love poems he had Todd deliver from Briarwood on his behalf). The most recent one had arrived yesterday, rolled into a tight scroll and tied to a bag of gummy bears. It said:

C,
They can expel you from OCD. But they can't kick you out of my HEART.
C

Todd had stolen the orange gummies, but she didn't care. Love made her a more forgiving person, even toward her brother.

Massie checked her watch, then knocked the phone out

of Claire's clammy palm. "Wait! Wouldn't you rather tell them in person?"

"Totally, but I'm grounded." Claire felt a pinch behind her eyes. "I'm not allowed to ride my bike."

"So, Isaac can drive you." Massie pulled the bobby pins out of her hair and shook her long, shiny extensions like she was auditioning for a Pantene commercial. "How long will it take you to get dressed?"

"Five seconds." Claire felt a tingle in her stomach. They were going to visit Cam. *Finally!*

"Can you do it in three? The mall closes at eight p.m. tonight." Massie stepped into her purple Uggs and black Juicy sweats. "I'll call the others. We'll meet at the Range Rover in twenty."

"Huh? Why the mall?" Even *saying* the word made Claire's chest tighten.

"To shop." Massie was halfway to the door.

"Are you still going to drop me off at Cam's?"

"Tomorrow."

"But you just said—"

"I meant tomorrow."

"But—"

"Um, are you part of the Pretty Committee or not?"

Claire nodded.

"Then you better look ah-mazing on Monday." Massie stuffed her hands in the side pockets of her white velour sweatshirt. "Your outfit needs to say Hollywood, *not* Hollywouldn't."

"But I can't afford anything. My parents took away my allowance."

"We'll find *something*." Massie put her arm around Claire's waist and gave a gentle squeeze. "Come on, it'll be fun. Besides, we have to prioritize."

Claire's heart felt like a leaking balloon. *I* was *prioritizing*, she wanted to say.

Instead, she sprinted back to the guesthouse and slipped on the "borrowed" Citizens, a gray ribbed turtleneck, and her black-and-white slip-on Keds. What choice did she have? Without Cam, Layne, or OCD, the Pretty Committee was all she had.

"Todd!" Claire called for the nine hundredth time. "Come on! This is stupid." She knocked her head against the cold rear window of the Range Rover and sighed. In two hours, the Pretty Committee would be face-to-face with Abby Boyd and Hadley Durk. She should be fixing her short bangs, not looking for her delinquent brother.

"Kuh-laire, forget about him." Massie smoothed her burgundy silk tunic. It was cinched at the waist with a wide tan belt and worn over a pair of superstraight jeans and matching tan ankle boots. "*The Daily Grind* starts at nine a.m. We have to leave ay-sap."

"I know . . . but this is my fault." Claire bit down on her chapped lip.

Massie turned and glared. "How?"

"I called him a loser because he has to go to school while I get to go to the show."

"How evil and un-Claire-ish. I love it." She checked her extensions in the side mirror. Jakkob had tied them into an ultrahigh genie pony, so it swung between her shoulder blades when she moved.

"It was his fault. He wet-burped milk while I was eating poached eggs and it almost made me barf."

"Then he deserved it. Can we go now?" Massie tapped on the side window. "Isaac, we're ready."

He stepped out of the SUV and clicked open the back door. A rush of heat escaped into the chilly wind, beckoning them to come inside.

"Dad, we have to go or we'll be late!" Claire yelled as she inched closer to the warmth. She wanted to help but thought it best to leave before he changed his mind. Besides, the moms were checking the houses. Someone would find Todd eventually. "Sorry. Good luck!"

"Thanks." Jay Lyons stroked his graying beard as he scanned the lawn. "Don't forget, you have a lot of history homework. And it better be done by the time I get home." A puff of air shot through his nostrils, making him look like a smoke-breathing dragon.

"It will be." Claire forced a smile and waved. "Promise."

Jay waved goodbye, then continued looking. "Come on, Todd, I'm late for a meeting!" He cupped his hands around his mouth and shouted, "Buddy, I have to take you to school whether you like it or not."

William Block was in his black Mercedes sedan, checking his watch and rubbing his bald head. If he was anything like his daughter, his patience had run out a half-hour ago.

"Bye, Daddy," Massie called from the backseat.

William rolled down his window. "Bye, sweetheart. Don't forget to ask a lot of questions. It's the best way to learn."

"I will. Say goodbye to Mom." She blew her father a kiss

as Isaac pulled out of the circular driveway. Her smile was so sugary sweet it almost gave Claire a zit.

"Who first?" Isaac glanced in the rearview mirror.

"Alicia, then Dylan, then Kristen." Massie pulled a CD out of her logo-embossed Gucci tote. "Can you play this?"

Isaac fed the CD into the car stereo.

"What is it?" Claire asked, trying to push the morning's drama out of her head.

"Abby Boyd's playlist from iTunes." Massie twirled her ponytail around her finger. "I haven't heard of any of the songs, but I bet it's awesome."

Claire sat back and bobbed her head to the screeching guitar riff that kicked off the first track.

"How much longer, Isaac?" Claire's temples were throbbing from thirty-seven minutes of blasting, angry, alternative chick rock.

"Two more songs!" he shouted.

"Ehmagawd," Alicia squealed as they rolled past the George Washington Bridge. "Abby Boyd and Hadley Durk are two songs away!"

"Does it have to be *these* songs?" Kristen whined.

"I'm telling Abby you said that," Dylan teased.

Claire giggled.

"Rate me out of ten." Massie leaned forward and put her hands on her hips like a model from a Macy's back-to-school ad.

"Nine-five," Dylan said to her compact mirror as she scraped a bran flake off her left molar.

Massie gave her friend a playful shove. "You're not even looking at me."

Dylan wiped the wet bran chunk under the seat. "We just rated you, like, five minutes ago."

"I know, but my makeup could have smudged since then." Massie applied what had to have been her eleventh coat of Glossip Girl Candy Apple lip gloss. It looked like her mouth had been sealed with saran wrap.

"You look better than I do." Kristen tightened the purple-and-blue Pucci scarf around her head, clearly hoping to add a touch of femininity to her slow-growing boy cut. "I'm wearing library clothes." She tugged her black Splendid sweats.

"I told you I would bring you something," Massie said.

"Puh-lease. If my mom asks me to send her another picture and I'm dressed up? Ehmagawd, I don't even!"

"Well, I give you a nine-eight," Claire offered. Even in sweats and a head scarf, Kristen looked downtown chic in that effortless sort of way. "You're all nine-eights."

Dylan was rodeo cute in gold cowboy boots, a pink corduroy mini, and a western shirt. And, as usual, Alicia looked like a Ralph Lauren model in her dark jeans, shrunken navy blazer, ivory cami, and knee-high riding boots.

"Really?" Kristen fastened the backs of her tiny silver hoop earrings. "A nine-eight?"

"Yup." Claire crossed her legs, obviously trying to hide the faint toothpaste stain above the knee on her cutoff cargos.

"Want us to rate you?" Alicia asked Claire's striped Keds.

"'Kay." Claire unzipped her jacket.

"First, what's with the capri pants?" Alicia asked.

"And the Keds without socks?" Dylan added.

"The black turtleneck is cute," Kristen noted. "A little snug, but cute."

"Actually, the Hermès scarf as a belt is a nice touch." Alicia clapped her hands.

"Thanks, it's mine." Massie bowed. "I was going for a South-of-France thing. The short bangs were my inspiration."

"*You* styled her?"

"Yup." Massie nodded. "Of course I gave her a pair of black Choo slides but she ahb-viously thought those Keds were nicer."

"The slides pinched my toes."

"Whatevs." Massie lifted a mascara wand to her lashes. "Did you charge the camera battery?"

"Yup."

"Perf." Massie grinned. "Once we mass e-mail a picture of us with Abby and Hadley, everyone, including the LBRs in Da Crew and the Country Club, will worship the Pretty Committee even more than they already do."

"I should have brought my tripod." Claire sighed, wishing she could be in the pictures too.

Alicia reached inside her oversize Marc Jacobs bag and

pulled out an iPod. She leaned forward and handed it to Claire. "Here. Use mine."

Kristen burst out laughing.

"Uh, thanks." Claire winked at Kristen, then took the thin white rectangle. This was probably not the best time to teach Alicia the difference between an iPod and a tripod.

The instant Isaac turned left off of Eighth Avenue and onto Twenty-sixth Street, they saw Merri-Lee Marvil's poreless face. It was plastered across the side of an old brick building along with the show's infamous logo—a steaming cup of coffee with *The Daily Grind* written in what was supposed to look like half-and-half.

"Stop the car, I have to get out." Dylan undid her seat belt and popped the top snap on her skirt.

"No one goes anywhere until I park," Isaac insisted.

Dylan dug her fingernails into the back of his seat. "Seriously, I have to go." She unlocked the doors.

"What are you doing?" Alicia gasped.

"I've got the thunda from down unda." Dylan's cheeks were flushed and her upper lip was beaded with sweat.

"So that bran diet is going well?" Massie smiled in an I-told-you-so sort of way.

Dylan kicked open the door and jumped out.

"*Dylan!*" Isaac slammed on the brakes.

But it was too late. She was already running toward the studio.

"Perfect landing." Massie applauded.

"How did she do that?" Claire tugged her bangs.

"Stunt double." Kristen giggled.

"Look at her." Alicia pointed. "She's running like a human gingerbread cookie. All stiff and side-to-side."

Even Isaac couldn't hide his smile.

"Ehmagawd." Kristen fanned her face and began bouncing up and down. "Across the street!"

"Ehmagawd!" the others shrieked. And at the exact same time, they lifted their cell phones and started snapping pictures of the black limousine parked a few feet away.

"They were in there. They were actually in there this morning. How awesome is that?" Kristen beamed.

"There's another one." Massie pointed. "Kuh-laire, are you getting this with the good camera?"

"Yup." She followed by snapping four shots, two on zoom and two wide.

This was really happening. So what if her bangs were short and her sweater was snug? She was about to meet Abby Boyd and Hadley Durk.

Isaac turned off the engine.

"Come on." Massie led the charge, and Alicia and Kristen followed. They faced the blustering wind without tights, coats, hats, scarves, or gloves. Claire, determined to do the same, wiggled out of her puffy jacket and tossed it on the seat. But the instant she stepped away from the toasty Range Rover, a bitter gust of wind sent her flying back to zip up.

"Kuh-laire, are you coming?" Massie shouted from halfway down the block.

Claire's insides warmed immediately. They were the kind of friends who waited for one another.

"Hurry!" Massie shouted.

"Coming!" Claire waved goodbye to Isaac and darted down the street.

"It's about time!" She smiled when Claire arrived.

"Sorry," Claire panted as she opened her jacket and draped its puffiness around Massie's shoulder. "Thanks for waiting."

"Of course I'm going to wait." Massie rolled her eyes. "I need you to photograph our entrance. And stay on my left side. It's more photogenic than my right."

"Oh." Claire slid the jacket off Massie's shoulder and wrapped it around herself, zipping it all the way to the top. She had gone from cool to cold in a matter of seconds.

The coffee-and-toast smell of Village Studios' stark lobby made Massie regret skipping breakfast—not that she could have gotten anything down even if she tried. Her stomach was locked and her nerves held the keys.

"Which way to the set?" she asked the frazzled, headset-wearing receptionist with the lipstick-stained can of chocolate Slim Fast on her desk.

"Village Studios, this is Joyce, please hold." She hit a button on the switchboard. "Village Studios, this is Joyce, please hold."

Massie twirled her gold charm bracelet and sighed.

"Village Studios, this is Joyce, please hold."

Massie tapped the top of Joyce's desk. "Um, excuse me, *Janet.* . . ."

Kristen and Alicia muffled their giggles.

"Which way is the studio? Merri-Lee Marvil is expecting us."

"Have a seat." Joyce pointed to the black leather couch in the waiting area. "Someone will be with you shortly." She poked her switchboard. "Village Studios, this is Joyce, please hold."

"Um, *Janet*, you may not realize this, but the show is live in, like, fifteen minutes, and we're supposed to meet Abby and Hadley be-*fore* they go on. Not after."

Joyce shooed Massie away as though she were a flea-infested cat.

"But our friend Dylan is waiting for us in there," Alicia pleaded. "Maybe you know her? She's Merri-Lee's *daughter*."

Joyce responded by swiveling her Herman Miller chair so that her back faced them.

"You are so dead to me." Massie made an X with her fingers, indicating that Joyce had severe split ends.

"She is so getting sued." Alicia fell back on the over-stuffed couch.

"Let's tell Merri-Lee to fire her." Massie sat.

"Do you think I could get her job?" Kristen asked.

Claire was about to sit too, when Massie lifted her right palm. "Hold!"

"What?"

"Can you get a shot of us in the waiting room?"

"Of course, your highness. I would be honored." Claire cocked her digital camera. "Anything for you."

Alicia and Kristen immediately turned to Massie.

"What? I thought you liked photography." She stroked her ponytail. "I thought this was the ultimate assignment for you. I *thought* you'd be excited."

"I am." Claire's expression softened. "Sorry." She raised the camera.

"Wait!" Massie lifted her palm again. "Kristen, let me switch places with you." She rolled directly across her friend's lap. "I have to be on the left."

"Ready?" Claire asked.

"Dial C for Cheese." Massie flashed a fabulous, toothy smile.

Then a stocky woman pushed through the glass doors with the grace of a linebacker in three-inch heels. A walkie-talkie was clipped to an empty belt loop on her black Levi's and a clipboard was nestled under her armpit. "Mayse Black plus three?"

"I think you mean Massie Block." Alicia giggled.

She shrugged.

The girls jumped to their feet.

"Follow me."

She led them down a gray-carpeted hallway, the walls filled with autographed head shots of former *Daily Grind* guests. "I'm Kay."

"O-Kay," Massie responded, deadpan.

"Yes?" Kay tucked her dry brown bangs behind her ear. "Did you have a question?"

"No, we're O-Kay." Alicia bit her lower lip, fighting a smile.

"Good." Kay sounded somewhat confused but satisfied. "Then let's make tracks."

Thanks to a pair of white Reeboks and zero interest in the celebrity photos, Kay was first to make it to the end of the corridor. She stood in front of the only door with a gleaming gold star in the center. Hadley's and Abby's names were engraved inside the star.

"Everyone decent?" Kay knocked.

The thumping bass of some unidentifiable rap song was all they heard.

Massie pinched Alicia's arm, Alicia pinched Kristen's, and Kristen pinched Claire's.

"This is the green room." Kay lowered her ear to the door. "Our guests hang out here before the show."

Claire lifted her Elph.

"Absolutely not." Kay smacked her hand. "Take one and we'll take your camera. Take two and we'll take your arm."

Massie rolled her eyes, letting Claire know Kay's threats were not to be taken seriously.

A muffled, static-filled voice broke the tension. "Kay, what's your twenty? Over."

She unclipped the walkie-talkie from her jeans and lifted it to her mouth. "I'm outside the green room. Over."

"Yeah, uh, we need some napkins in the control room aysap. Over."

"Copy that. Over." She started bolting down the hall, then turned back to the girls. "Go on in. I'll be back in a jiff."

"Can she just leave us like that?" Alicia checked her reflection in the gold star.

"That is so not O-Kay." Kristen adjusted her Pucci head scarf.

Claire turned off the flash on her camera and took a picture of her friends laughing.

"Dare me?" Massie put her hand on the brass doorknob.

"Do it," Alicia whispered.

But Massie quickly pulled away. "I can't!"

"Come awn," Alicia urged.

"Open it," Kristen begged.

"You!"

"I'll do it." Claire pushed past the girls and grabbed the knob. "Maybe this time one of you could take *my* picture?"

"Take a picture of this!" Massie shoved her out of the way and pushed open the door. The smell of roses and vanilla-scented candles flooded the hall.

"It's not *green*," Alicia whispered in Massie's ear. "It's beige-ish."

I can see that, Massie wanted to say. But she was paralyzed from the forehead down and couldn't speak. Not that anyone would have heard her if she had tried.

An electronic remix of Pink's "Stupid Girls" raged at top volume from a pair of Visa-thin speakers, rousing a skinny, fur-vest-wearing bleached-blond guy to leap onto the L-shaped couch and gyrate to the beat. Two brunettes in identical True Religion jeans cast their coffee cups aside and danced at his feet. An assortment of pillar and votive candles were on every available surface, casting long shadows on the walls as several agents, managers, and assistants paced back and forth, shouting into their cell phones. An elaborate assortment of baked goods, fresh fruit, and watermelon-flavored Jolly Ranchers dominated the round glass table near the uniformed bartender, who was doling out fresh smoothies and cappuccino. What was supposed to be a holding area for guests of the show looked more like a trendy New York City nightclub.

Massie scanned the frenetic scene, her heart beating to the pounding rhythm of the remix.

"I don't see them," Alicia said with a trace of panic.

"Be cool, okay? These people can't think we're pathetic fans."

"But we are." Kristen dropped her stuffed book bag on the floor, and Massie quickly kicked it under the red table-cloth draped over the food table. She followed up with a don't-even-think-about-picking-that-ridiculous-thing-up-until-we-leave look.

"No way!" Claire gasped, her mouth hanging open like Cam was about to feed her a fistful of gummy worms. Without another word she marched across the room, pushing her way through the well-dressed crowd.

"Kuh-laire, get back here!" Massie whisper-shouted. "We should all go together."

But Claire refused to stop.

"Let's go." Massie grabbed Alicia and Kristen. "She's heading for the couch."

"Ehmagawd." Alicia stopped. Massie dragged her forward the same way she dragged Bean when the puppy didn't want to go for a walk in the cold.

"Stop." Alicia pointed to the actresses, who were sitting on the floor by the white leather couch. "Look!"

"It's a massage train." Kristen fixed her narrow aqua eyes on the spectacle.

"And look who's riding it!" Massie didn't know whether to laugh or call the authorities.

Hadley Durk was the caboose, kneading a younger boy's shoulders. And the boy, who was in the middle, was karate-chopping Abby Boyd's neck.

"You are so dead!" Claire shouted.

"Funny, I don't feel dead." The boy turned his head and winked at Hadley. It was Todd Lyons.

"How much do you *love* this guy?" Hadley twirled one of her signature Pocahontas braids and chuckled. Her brown, almond-shaped eyes narrowed and her flawless skin glowed. She looked airbrushed.

"Ehmagawd, you're even prettier in real life," Kristen blurted.

Massie immediately elbowed her in the rib cage.

"Thanks." Hadley smiled, flashing her Dentyne Ice–shaped teeth.

"Todd, how did you get here?" Claire demanded, completely oblivious to the actresses.

"I was hiding in the back of the Range Rover. When Isaac went to the bathroom, I hopped out and snuck in the side door with the Poland Spring delivery dude."

"How funny is that?" Abby slapped her knee; the gold bangles on her left arm backed her up with a clang. She was wearing a yellow chiffon dress over straight-legged black velvet pants. A fedora shaded her hazel eyes.

"It's pretty funny." Claire turned bright red, as if she finally realized who she was talking to. Then she hovered above the actress and stared, her face frozen in a wide smile, as if some cosmic pause button had been hit while she was posing for a picture.

"That's my poor sister, Claire." Todd lowered his voice to a sympathetic whisper. "She was born with this weird disease that makes her freeze up whenever she pees in her pants."

"What?" Claire stomped her foot. "Don't listen to *him*." She turned red again.

"It's okay," Todd said kindly. "No one is making fun of you."

Abby and Hadley lowered their heads, obviously trying to conceal their grins.

"I'm calling Dad." Claire waved her scratched Nokia in Todd's face, then turned on the heels of her Keds and stormed into the hallway.

Massie rolled her eyes, silently distancing herself from Claire's uptight behavior and cheap cell phone. She cleared her throat. "Hey, I'm Massie."

"I *know* who you are." Todd grimaced. "We used to have a thing, remember?"

"Ew." Massie smacked the top of his head. "We did nawt!"

"Nice to meet you." Abby waved. Her nails were painted navy blue, and each of her fingers was adorned with a different hard-to-miss cocktail ring. "Massie, right?"

She nodded. Hearing her name come out of Abby's mouth

was borderline creepy. It was like the actress's red-carpet shot had come to life and started talking to her from the pages of *Us Weekly*. It made Massie shudder with a kind of eerie excitement.

"Hi, I'm Alicia and this is Kristen."

"Hhh-eyyyy." Abby's voice vibrated as Todd's karate chops began working their way down her spine.

"Hi." Hadley tugged on one of her eyelashes, then wiped her finger on the white couch, leaving behind a mascara skid mark.

"So, are you guys contest winners or something?" Abby inspected their outfits. "Is that why you're here?"

"Ew, no." Massie winced. "We're tight with Merri-Lee. We come to all the shows."

"Don't you have school?" Hadley wondered.

"We dropped out." Massie immediately glared at Todd, warning him to keep his mouth shut.

"Cool!" Abby snapped her fingers two times.

"Why?" Hadley seemed genuinely curious. "I kind of miss going to school."

"Uh, modeling."

"Really?" Abby was suddenly interested. "Fashion or editorial?"

"Yup."

Massie quickly stepped aside, making room for Claire, who had just squeezed through the cluster of managers and agents to rejoin the conversation.

"Todd, Isaac is in the lobby, waiting to take you home. If

you don't leave now, the security guard in the hall will be happy to escort you."

"Fine." Todd slowly pushed himself up and blew a kiss to each of the girls. "Let's stay in touch." He grabbed an umbrella-adorned smoothie off the glass coffee table and bit down on the straw.

"Definitely." Hadley stood and hugged him goodbye. She was wearing a denim micromini, gray knee-highs, and a tight red T-shirt that spelled out J'ADORE GABOR in silver studs.

"Good luck with your TV series." Abby crawled onto the couch and brought her knees to her chest. "I'll totally watch for it." She snapped her fingers twice.

Claire rolled her eyes. "Go!" She pushed Todd toward the door and watched, hands on her hips, until he was gone.

Massie exchanged a quick glance with Alicia. Did Claire not see the two movie stars? Did she not care that Abby Boyd and Hadley Durk would think she was an uptight goody-goody? Why did she have to act like such a mom?

"Cute Sue," Hadley noted.

Everyone followed her eyes. She was pointing at Claire's black-and-white striped Keds.

"I said, cute shoes!" she shouted over the music. "Look." She wiggled her left ankle. "I have the same ones."

Massie's forehead began breaking out in a sweat.

"No way!" Claire shot Massie a how-do-you-like-me-now? look.

She shot a look back that said, *You're still not cool.*

"Does this make us sole mates?" Claire beamed.

"Ehmagawd!" Massie covered her face with her hands. "You did nawt just say that!"

"Effing genius!" Hadley bounced up and down on her toes. "Did you make that up?"

Claire nodded slowly, probably wondering if it was a trap.

"Can I use it sometime?" Hadley put her hands together in prayer.

"Sure," Claire said directly to Massie. "Anytime."

"So, Hadley." Massie stepped in front of Claire. "Is it true?"

"Is what true?" Hadley lifted a plate of chocolate-covered strawberries off the glass coffee table by the couch.

"You and Gabor?" Massie pointed to her T-shirt.

Abby giggle-snorted.

"What?" Hadley asked, obviously confused.

"Nothing," Abby said as she pulled a large red stone off one of her cocktail rings. She dipped her pinky inside and lifted out a glob of sparkle-infused gloss, which she dabbed on her full lips.

"Gabor and I have been in love since Christmas." Hadley popped a strawberry into her mouth.

While Massie was nodding, pretending to follow the story, she pinched Claire's wrist and murmured, "Picture" from the side of her mouth. Claire snapped a quick shot.

Kristen and Alicia rushed to either side of Hadley, hoping

to be in the next one, but Massie growled and they backed away.

"Next weekend we're going to the Swiss Alps so he can show me the resort that put his picture on the lift tickets."

"You're so lucky," Kristen chimed in. "I would love to date a pro snowboarder. They have the most ah-mazing clothes."

"And they're faithful." Hadley sighed, "I'm over dating actors. All they do is cheat." She glared at Abby.

"Ew! What is *that*?" Abby pointed at the floor. "It's revolsive!"

Everyone knew about Abby Boyd's vocabulary, otherwise known as the "a-bby-c's." She had been making up her own ah-mazing words in magazine interviews and on talk shows for as long as Massie could remember.

"It looks like a ferret." Hadley sounded amused.

Abby snapped her fingers in agreement.

Alicia, Claire, and Kristen burst out laughing. They knew exactly what that "revolsive" thing on the floor was.

"Um, I think you dropped your weave." Abby pinched the long brown extension and laid it on Massie's shoulder.

"Thanks." Massie rolled her eyes, trying to quell the tornado of humiliation that was swirling inside of her. *Why this? Why now?* This was supposed to be an "OMG" moment, the moment when Abby Boyd found her future BFF, Massie Block . . . not her hair.

"My stylist is so fired!" She dropped the extension in her Gucci and turned away to hide her burning cheeks.

"I hear ya." Abby's smile was sympathetic. "I had those stupid extensions for a while. Then it hit me." She snapped once. "Long brown hair is so commonstream. So I axed it."

She took off her fedora and tousled a new short blond Sienna Miller 2006 cut. It was the exact opposite of the dark, rib-dusting 'do she'd sported in *Us Weekly*.

"Ehmagawd," Massie heard herself say. "When?"

"Tuesday."

"Hey." Alicia smacked Massie's arm. "Isn't that the same day you put yours in?"

Massie nodded, wondering if Alicia's lawyer dad could sue the trashy tabloid for printing old photos.

"I did the same thing." Kristen pulled off her Pucci head scarf and flaunted her boy cut.

"Ehmagawd!" Massie wanted to scream. Kristen *hated* her hair!

"Don't you feel so much more sophisticated?" Abby lifted her wrist to her mouth and bit into her pastel-colored candy bracelet.

"Totally." Kristen fluffed her uneven layers. "Ever since I got this cut, people think I'm fifteen."

"And a guy." Massie couldn't help herself.

Alicia and Hadley burst out laughing. Kristen's cheeks turned bright red.

"Heyyyyy." Dylan inserted herself into the conversation. "Wha'd I miss?" A red curl was stuck to her lip gloss.

"Abby and I have matching haircuts." Kristen beamed.

"And look at Hadley's shoes." Claire pointed. "We have the same Keds."

"Ah-dorable!" Dylan shouted. "You *have* to show my mom. It's like that special she did called 'Bankrupt and Beautiful,' about regular people who spend their savings to look like celebrities. She won an Emmy for that."

Massie rolled her eyes. Dylan was ahb-viously showing off.

"How do you feel?" she smirked. "Did you make it to the bathroom in time?"

"Yup." Dylan didn't seem the least bit embarrassed. "Glad that's over." She grabbed her butt cheeks. "I had to grow a tail in the biggest way."

"Ew!" Alicia cracked up.

Hadley dropped her plate of strawberries on the glass coffee table.

"Sorry." Massie apologized on Dylan's behalf. "She didn't mean to—"

"Did you just say 'grow a tail'?" Hadley knit her arched eyebrows.

"Yeah." Dylan giggled.

"That is so effing genius." Hadley high-fived her. "Gabor is going to love that!" She whipped out her Motorola Sidekick and began thumbing the keypad at top speed.

"Classic." Abby snapped three times.

"Isn't it?" Massie tried to laugh with them. But nothing came out.

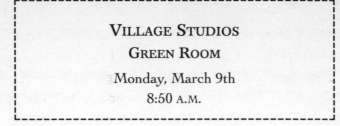

"Audio!" shouted a scruffy blond dude in a faded New York University tee. He was in the center of the bustling green room craning his neck. "Abby? Hadley?"

Claire tapped Hadley's bony shoulder. "I think that guy's looking for you."

"Meow!" Abby shoved Hadley aside. "Over here, cowboy." She waved.

With a quick nod, he hurried toward her.

"He looks more like Mickey Mouse in those big headphones," Claire said.

Everyone cracked up except Massie.

"I'm Erik." He sounded out of breath. "I need to get these mics on you. We're live in ten minutes."

He ran a thin wire up Hadley's J'ADORE GABOR shirt, then clipped a tiny round microphone to her collar. "Thanks." She smiled.

His cheeks flushed.

"My turn." Abby stuck out her chest like he was their plastic surgeon. "You are too cute. And I never go for blonds." She grinned. "Tell me you're single and I'll stuff you in my Balenciaga and take you back to Beverly Hills."

"Ehmagawd, I have a Balenciaga too!" Dylan beamed.

"It's right over—" She started spinning in circles like a dog chasing its tail. "Ehmagawd, it's gone! I must have left it in the bathroom." Her panic-filled eyes begged for help.

Unsure of what a Balenciaga was or how to react when one goes missing, Claire plopped down on the white couch, hoping her ignorance would go unnoticed.

"I'll find it," Massie volunteered, probably to show Abby and Hadley what a good friend she was.

"Let me help." Alicia raced to Massie's side.

"I'll wait here." Claire brought her knees to her chest, the way Abby had earlier.

"Me too." Kristen joined her.

Massie hooked her thumbs through her belt loops. "I think you should come with us."

"It's cool, they can hang." Hadley twirled one of her braids.

Claire smiled graciously.

"No," Massie snapped. "It's not."

Claire and Kristen exchanged a glance.

"I'm serious." Massie stomped her foot. "Dylan needs us right now."

The girls exchanged another glance while Massie stood above them tapping her foot. Alicia's arms were folded across her C-cups.

"You're right." Kristen pulled herself up to stand.

Claire sighed and did the same. She was too embarrassed to say goodbye to Hadley and hurried off.

"I don't understand why we *all* have to go." Kristen

pulled her book bag out from under the food table and followed Massie into the hall.

"Because we're BFFs and we help each other in emergencies."

"Point," Alicia sneered.

"Sorry," Kristen murmured.

"Found it!" Dylan shouted when the girls entered the bathroom. She was leaning against the silver trough sink, cradling the red leather bag like she had just birthed it from her loins.

"Cool, now can we go back?" Claire gripped the door handle.

"No," Dylan whispered. "Close it. Close it."

"Why?" She stepped back inside.

"I have some news that's worth at least, hmmmmm." Dylan bit her lip and searched the ceiling. "One thousand gossip points."

"Shut up!" Alicia slapped her arm. "I only got five hundred for 'Lara Davis pees her bed.' And there's no way yours can beat *that*."

Dylan stuck out her hand. "Bets?"

Massie swatted her hand away.

"I'll decide when I hear it."

"Okay, so after I grew a tail, I went to say hi to Sheena, my mom's stylist." Dylan started off whispering but quickly returned to her regular tone. "And she told me that Abby was on her Sidekick, like, the *entire* time she was getting her hair done."

Massie fake-yawned. "Borrr-ing."

Everyone cracked up.

"Stop laughing." Dylan punched her Balenciaga. "That's ahb-viously not the best part."

"Hurry up, then." Kristen checked her cell phone. "The show is live in, like, three minutes."

Dylan took a deep breath, then continued. "So, Sheena saw that Abby got an e-mail from her friend Suki, who asked if she hooked up with Gabor after their date last night."

"Wait, isn't Gabor Hadley's boyfriend?" Claire asked.

"Ex-actly!" Dylan gave her a playful shove, accidentally knocking Claire into the tampon dispenser.

"Ehmagawd, so what did Abby say?" Alicia flapped her hands like a cuckoo bird in flight. "Did she hook up with Gabor?"

"Abby wrote back, 'Of course we hooked up, we always do.'"

Everyone's mouths hung open, but no one said a word.

"It turns out Abby and Gabor have been hooking up behind Hadley's back for *weeks*."

"Ehmagawd, first Palmer, now Gabor!" Alicia pounded her fist on the steel trough.

"Abby is pathological." Kristen sounded disgusted.

Claire wondered if anyone knew what *pathological* meant, but everyone nodded in agreement so she did too.

"You totally earned your gossip points." Massie whipped out her PalmPilot and added one thousand to Dylan's score.

"All personnel to the studio floor. We are live in two minutes," a deep male voice announced over the PA system.

Suddenly, a toilet flushed.

Claire's spine stiffened. Gossip rule number one is: Never dish in a public bathroom. Even *she* knew that.

"Ehmagawd." Dylan fanned her mouth like she had just bitten into a chili pepper.

"Run!" Massie whisper-yelled.

"Not to worry, girlies, your secret's safe with me." Calgary Edwards, Merri-Lee's ah-nnoyingly perky cohost, raced out of the stall as though flames were shooting out of the bowl. She pumped some L'Occitane Verbena Harvest soap, turned the faucet with her elbow, and scrubbed vigorously. "I'm a vault." She shook the water off her hands, then hurried out.

The girls burst out laughing the second she was gone.

"One minute to live, folks," the voice announced. *"Places."*

"Ehmagawd, the show's about to start!" Kristen tossed her book bag under the trough.

"Follow me." Dylan grabbed Massie's wrist and led everyone through a maze of hallways. She parted two heavy black curtains and suddenly, voilà!—they were on the set of *The Daily Grind*.

"Wow," was all Claire could say. She had spent hundreds of mornings watching Merri-Lee and her guests chat about movies, music, and fashion from *The Daily Grind*'s famous rotating stage. And now she was *there*, close enough to touch it.

Everything looked the way it did on TV, only smaller. As expected, the panoramic photo of the New York skyline hung behind Merri-Lee's desk. Her cappuccino cart was in arm's reach of her leopard-print wing chair, and the guest couch was covered in white faux fur. The flat-screen monitor she used to interview her guests on the West Coast was getting a quick spray-down with Windex, but other than that, it looked the same too. The only thing that seemed different was the audience applause. It was ten times louder in person, especially once the band busted into the show's jazzy theme. Everyone put down their complimentary coffee, jumped to their feet, and started dancing. Claire shook her hips, wishing Cam could see.

"Kuh-laire, we're VIPs!" Massie hissed. "Stop acting like *them*." She tilted her head toward the audience.

"Sorry." She stopped moving and did her best to look bored and unimpressed.

"Ready, girlies?" Calgary smoothed her sexy tan business suit.

"Ready!" Claire responded as if they were about to take the stage together.

"'Scuse me, Calgary?" Erik, the scruffy audio guy, gently placed a hand on her back. "Remember to turn your microphone off when you use the ladies' room. You are patched through to the house speakers, and we can hear—"

"Oh no." Calgary smacked her own forehead. "Could everyone on the studio floor hear me tinkle?"

He lowered his head and nodded.

"IT'SSSSS *THE DA-ILY GRIIIIIND!*" the show's announcer roared.

The audience exploded with applause.

"THE WEEKEND IS FINALLY OVER, AND IT'S TIME TO GET DOWN TO SOME SERIOUS BUSINESS!"

That was Calgary's cue. She strode on set swinging her emerald-green alligator briefcase.

"She is so busted," Massie said into her cupped hands.

The girls giggled into their palms, tears gathering in their eyes.

"Imagine if she had the thunda from down unda?" Dylan burst out into hysterics.

"We wouldn't have to imagine," Alicia snorted. "We'd hear it."

They cracked up even harder.

"Ehmagawd, look." Kristen's smile faded.

They followed her gaze to the watercooler on the side of the set and saw Hadley jumping up and down on Abby's gray fedora.

Massie twirled her long ponytail. "Serves Abby right for cutting her hair!"

"That hat belonged to my grandfather!" Abby shouted. "Give it!" She tugged one of Hadley's braids. "Back!" She tugged the other.

"Well, Gabor was *my* boyfriend." Hadley kicked Abby's shin.

She grabbed her leg. "You can have him. He kisses like a snapping turtle."

"AND NOW FOR EVERYONE'S FAVORITE BOSS, MERRI-LEE MARVIL!"

Dylan's mom bounded onto the set from the far side of the stage. Her red wavy hair bounced with every step she took. She blew kisses to her fans, completely unaware of her feuding guests. Once she was seated in her leopard-print chair, Merri-Lee held her yellow mug in front of her lips and waited for the audience to quiet down.

"The show is starting." Claire tugged Massie's tunic.

"Puh-lease. This is way more exciting than *The Daily Grind*. It's an *Us Weekly* cover in the making. Quick, where's your camera?"

"*No pictures!*" Kay, the production assistant, appeared out of nowhere.

"How could you do this to me *again*?" Hadley smacked the top of the watercooler, her cheeks streaked with mascara.

"Stop being so dramantic." Abby popped open her blue ring and checked her reflection in the tiny mirror inside. "Anyway . . ." She snapped it shut. "You can't prove anything."

"Yes I can," Hadley continued, sobbing. "I heard those girls talking about it in the bathroom. Everyone in the whole studio heard the news, thanks to Calgary's microphone!"

"I must have missed that," Abby smirked. "While I was in the photo booth having text-sex with your boyfriend."

Hadley charged headfirst into her stomach.

"Ooph!" Abby grabbed her abs and gasped for air.

"Now put your hands together for the stars of the upcoming feature *Dial L for Loser*, Hadley Durk and Abby Boyd!" Merri-Lee stood and applauded.

"Now!" Kay nudged the girls toward the set, ignoring their scuffle. "Hurry!"

"You might as well take this." Hadley pulled off her J'ADORE GABOR shirt and whipped it at Abby's head.

"Maybe if you did that more often, Gabor wouldn't have cheated on you!" Abby shouted.

"Ladies, we're live!" Kay shouted. "Go! Go!"

"*Hadley Durk and Abby Boyd!*" Merri-Lee repeated, her eyes searching the set.

Hadley folded her arms across her black demi-cup bra.

"*Now!*" shouted Kay.

"I can't go out like *this*!" Hadley stood firm in her striped Keds.

Kay nudged her. "You should have thought of that before! We're *live*! Now *go!*"

"I am so not going out there with that illiterate man-eater," Hadley insisted.

"Yes! You! Are!" Kay shoved the shirtless actress onto the set, then circled back for Abby.

Once they were both on the rotating stage, Kay rested her head in her hands, shoulders shaking.

"Well, talk about a publicity stunt." Merri-Lee smiled awkwardly as beads of sweat congregated above her top lip.

"This isn't a publicity stunt, Merri-Lee." Hadley snapped

her own bra strap. Her eyes were puffy and her cheeks looked like they'd been slapped by a wet oil painting. "I *gave* Abby my shirt before the show."

"Why, might I ask?" Merri-Lee winked at the camera, letting the home audience know she was on the case.

Abby put her arm around Hadley like they were full-on BFFs. "Because our characters in the movie go to a party in their bras, and—"

"This has nothing to do with *Dial L* and you know it." Hadley turned her back to Abby.

"Don't do this." Abby placed a hand on her shoulder but Hadley shrugged it away.

Massie, Dylan, Alicia, Kristen, and Claire grabbed one another's wrists as tears gathered in Hadley's eyes.

"This is so intense." Kristen swallowed.

"Shhhhh," everyone hissed.

"Abby stole my boyfriend. *Again!*" Hadley spoke directly to the camera.

The audience gasped.

"Explain how Gabor sticking his tongue down my larynx at an animal rights benefit is *me* stealing *him*?"

Merri-Lee forced a laugh, like a seasoned anchorwoman. "Unfortunately, we have to take a break, but when we get back, celebrity chef Rolo DiSanto will teach the girls how to make tofu lasagna."

"Dial L for Lasagna," Massie blurted from the side of her mouth.

The girls cracked up.

"Sounds delicious." Calgary air-rubbed her stomach and licked her lips.

"Don't go anywhere. We'll be right back." Merri-Lee held her smile as the show's theme music began playing and the stage manager signaled the audience to cheer. When he lowered his arms, the applause died. So did Merri-Lee's smile.

"Will someone please tell me what the hell is going on here?"

Kay raced to the set with Hadley's red studded shirt. Seconds later, the stars were surrounded by a mass of hysterical producers.

"This cahn't be happening," declared a male with an ah-dorable British accent.

Massie turned around and locked eyes with Rupert Mann, the director of *Dial L for Loser*, whom she immediately recognized as number three on *People* magazine's "Ten Hottest Bachelors in Hollywood" list. He ran a hand through his ink-black hair, pushing his too-long-on-purpose bangs out of his cobalt-blue eyes.

"A deep tan and a good night's sleep and he could have *easily* made number one," Dylan whispered.

"Point," Alicia said.

Rupert unwrapped a stick of Big Red and folded it into his mouth.

"Hi," Massie blurted by accident.

"Do I know you?" he asked, unwrapping another stick of gum.

"Uh . . ." Massie paused, her mind racing. "Yeah, I was an extra in *Hurry Up and Wait*. I'm Massie, remember?"

"Roit, roit, of cose." He ran a hand through his thick black hair.

Claire suddenly remembered why everyone worshiped Massie Block. She was totally fearless.

Boop-boop.

Boop-boop.

Rupert reached into the front pocket of his Diesels and answered his phone.

"Of cou-ss I sawr it, you twit," he spit. "The enti-a flippin' country sawr it. . . . Hold on, I've got anotha call. . . . Hullo . . . Yes, I sawr it. . . . I know we start shooting in a week. Don't you think I know that? . . . Hold awn, I've got anotha call. . . . Hullo . . ."

"'Scuse me." A chubby production assistant in a white apron squeezed by with a silver cart of ingredients. He positioned it on set between Hadley and Abby.

"What do you think they're saying out there?" Claire asked.

"Only one way to find out." Massie suddenly pulled her onto the set.

"What are you doing?" Claire pretended to struggle, in case anyone was watching.

"Puh-lease. Do you really think anyone is paying attention to *us*?"

She had a point.

The producers, managers, and agents were too busy

shouting at one another to notice that Hadley was slicing the air with an uncooked lasagna noodle.

"You're crazy!" Abby shook her head in utter disbelief.

"Oh, *I'm* crazy?" Hadley lurched forward and poked Abby's arm with the noodle's sharp corner.

"*Ouch!*"

Then she stuck her hand in the Pyrex bowl of shredded mozzarella.

"Don't even think about it!" Abby warned.

"Okay, I won't!" Hadley whipped a fistful of white cheese at her face.

Abby gripped the bowl of tomato sauce.

"Ehmagawd." Claire lifted her hand to her mouth.

"This is history in the making." Massie watched in awe. "Take a picture."

"Don't even think about it!" Kay hissed as she hurried by.

"*We're back in twenty seconds,*" announced the deep voice over the PA system. Massie and Claire ran back to their seats.

"Throw that at me and I am so off this movie." Hadley put her hands on her hips and stood still.

"Promise?" Abby lifted the bowl.

"*We're back in ten.*"

"Oh, I promise." Hadley squinted, legs planted firmly.

"Hey, everyone!" Abby shouted. "Meet Chef Boyar-Hadlee." She lifted the bowl of tomato sauce and dumped it on Hadley's head.

"Awww, bloody 'ell!" Rupert whipped his phone onto the studio floor. It split wide open. "Bloody, bloody 'ell!" He kicked it across the floor. A pregnant audience member waddled out and scooped the phone off the ground. She lifted it above her head and her section broke into applause.

"*In three . . . two . . .*" The stage manager pointed at Merri-Lee as the audience cheered. They were back on the air.

"I'm done!" Hadley stormed off the set. "Good luck finding someone who will work with *her.*"

Like a true professional, Merri-Lee made no mention of Hadley and focused all of her attention on Abby as if she had been the only guest all along.

Massie lifted her Motorola and snapped a picture of the sauce-covered actress as she ran by.

"May I?" Rupert plucked the phone from her hand.

"Sure." Massie nudged Claire, who immediately took three shots of her grinning next to the red-faced director while he screamed, "What the bloody 'ell do I do now?" into her crystal-covered Motorola.

"Who is responsible for this?" He shouted with such force that a gob of spit landed on the mouthpiece. "Find me that person! I want that person!"

Dylan slowly backed away, then took off toward the rear exit.

Seconds later, Rupert stormed out of the studio, taking Massie's beloved phone with him.

"Look at all these flowers." Alicia tightened her black satin robe as she bent over a Jonathan Adler vase and sniffed an enormous bouquet of pink roses. "Are you sick or something?"

Massie rolled down the waistband on her white satin pajama bottoms. "My public misses me. Can you blame them?"

"You're like a celebrity." Claire plugged her Elph into Massie's computer. One by one, pictures from their morning at *The Daily Grind* appeared on-screen.

"Today Westchester, tomorrow the world!" Massie stroked Bean as she mentally marked the pictures she was going to include in her first-ever Pretty Committee newsletter. The mass e-mail would be the most effective way to stay in the hearts and minds of the wannabes at OCD, now that daily face time was no longer an option.

"I like the one of us outside Village Studios, the shot of me and Hadley, the shot of me and Rupert. That's probably it. The rest are too dark." Massie shook her new bottle of Naughty Navy nail polish, wishing Abby and Hadley could see her now.

Flower arrangements and gift baskets with cards

begging for her speedy return to OCD filled the nook by her bay window. Balloons were tied to the bedposts, and a menagerie of "Missing You" stuffed animals added a warm splash of color to elegant white furniture. Even without the gifts, the walk-in closet, forty-two-inch flat-screen TV, marble bathroom, and life-size mannequins of her and Bean would have rivaled the amenities available in the finest hotel suites in the world. And maybe, just maybe, if Abby and Hadley could have seen all this they would have been a little less interested in Claire and a lot more interested in her.

"Is that it?" Claire asked as she dragged the three shots onto the newsletter Massie had drafted earlier that afternoon.

"I guess." Massie pouted. "I wish there were better shots of you guys."

"I know," Alicia whined.

"At least you're in the picture in front of the studio," Claire said. "I'm not in any of them."

"I gave you photo credit." Massie pointed at the screen. "See?"

Claire nodded as she examined her microscopic shout-out at the bottom of the page.

    THE PRETTY COMMITTEE NEWSLETTER
      Hey! Thanks times ten for the ah-dorable gifts. We heart them all, especially the you-know-what from you-know-who. ☺

Everyone has been calling and e-mailing asking what we've been up to. So here's a summary of our week.

Monday: Hung out with Abby Boyd, Hadley Durk, and Rupert Mann (who borrowed my phone and never gave it back) on the set of *The Daily Grind*. Best time! (See pictures below.) The fight was in-sane. You ahb-viously read about it by now. OMG!

Tuesday: Spent most of the day with Hadley. She was so upset about Gabor. Sorry, I pinky-swore I wouldn't say more than that.

Wednesday: Shopped in NYC with Abby, Alicia, Kristen, Dylan, and Claire. Mostly Fifth Ave. Did you know that Abby brings her iPod to stores so they can play her favorite songs while she shops? I'll ask her if I can forward the playlist. It was awesome. We were dancing all day.

Thursday: Spa day at home with the girls.

Friday: Lunch with the girls at Dad's golf club, then snack shopping for Friday night sleepover.

The girls are here now and everyone says hi. How is school? Any tests?

Have fun! We know we will.

Love, Your Pretty Committee

MASSIE   DYLAN

Claire   KRISTEN   Alicia

*Photos by Claire Lyons.

"What's with the whole 'you-know-what from you-know-who'?" Claire asked. "What did you get?"

"Nothing," Massie smirked. "I made that up."

"You made it all up, didn't you?" Alicia asked.

"Well, do you remember shopping with Abby?"

"No."

"We're fighting a war here." Massie selected her newsletter-distribution list, and sixty-seven names appeared in her address bar. "Imagine going back to OCD and finding Da Crew at our lunch table. Or the Country Club under our tree." She hit send.

"That is, *if* we get back to school." Kristen threw down her *Philosophy for Dummies* book.

"Can I try these prunes?" Dylan poked the cellophane on a fruit-and-nut basket.

"Puuurp," Alicia teased, making a farting noise with her mouth.

Dylan slapped the back of her pink sweats. "Quiet down there."

"Ew!" Massie giggled. "Go for it." She flipped onto her stomach and began applying a fresh coat of Naughty Navy. Bean curled up beside her leg.

"I can't believe you're using Abby's nail polish color after what she did to Hadley." Kristen snapped the elastic band on her gray boy shorts.

"Oh, did Abby have this polish?" Massie widened her amber eyes.

"You didn't notice?"

"Nope." She dipped the brush and swished it around.

"Then why are you suddenly wearing navy?"

"I, um, got it in a gift basket."

"Whatevs." Kristen rolled her eyes.

"When did you start caring about Hadley anyway?" Alicia unrolled her puffy gold sleeping bag beside Massie's.

"I just feel bad for her. It's gotta suck having your boyfriend stolen."

"Funny." Dylan chewed a prune. "I thought you'd be on Abby's side because you both have such 'sophisticated' short hairdos." She lifted her mass of red curls and stumbled around the room like a runway model with a broken heel.

"Ow-chhh!" Her performance was cut short when she accidentally stepped in a bowl of Baked Lays. A prune chunk flew out of her mouth and landed on Massie's white duvet cover. "These chips are like razor blades!"

Kristen let out a cackle.

"Ew, Dylan." Massie didn't know whether to laugh or barf. "Clean that up."

"Sorry." She giggled on her way to the bathroom.

Bing.

"Massie, your computer." Claire jumped to her feet and pushed back the sleeves on her Powerpuff Girls pj's.

"Coming." Massie blew on her wet nails.

"It's Derrington!" Claire yelled. "SHORTZ4LIFE has invited you to an iChat. Should I respond?"

"Not if you like your arms in their sockets," Massie snapped.

"Hurry!" Claire bounced.

Massie pushed her aside and grabbed the wireless mouse.

"Is Josh with them?" Alicia padded over to the desk.

"Gawd, are you a couple of bulls?" Massie asked, shaking the mouse into place.

"No," Claire and Alicia said at the same time.

"Then why are you acting so horny?"

Massie finger-combed her extensions and searched her desk for a tube of Glossip Girl. She knocked Fettuccine Alfredo to the floor, grabbed Brown Sugar, and gave her lips a quick swipe.

"Kristen, grab a bunch of those vases and put them behind me."

"I can't right now." Kristen was struggling with her tangled jeans. "I don't want them to see me in my underwear."

"Alicia!"

"In a sec," she called from Massie's vanity, where she was braiding her hair like Hadley's.

"I got it." Claire's arms were full of bouquets and gift baskets.

Once the area behind Massie was suitably packed with baskets, balloons, and flowers, Massie adjusted the webcam on top of her monitor, then clicked accept. Derrington, Cam, and Josh were leaning against a red couch in Derrington's basement. The TV was on mute behind them.

"Nice newsletter, Block." Derrington twisted the cuffs on

his navy skate shorts. Josh and Cam were on either side of him, staring at their feet.

"Thanks." Massie scanned his outfit. *Yes!* He was wearing the rhinestone *M* brooch she'd given him last month. It was pinned to the sleeve of his light blue T-shirt, right above the chocolate stain.

"Is all that stuff true?" A dirty-blond curl fell into his eyes. He jerked his head, but it didn't move.

"What stuff?" Massie's heart quickened.

"Those rumors we've been hearing."

"Like what?" She took a deep breath and held it. Had word gotten out that they were responsible for Abby and Hadley's latest feud? Would everyone turn against them for causing Hadley to walk off *Dial L for Loser*? Had Claire told them she was more popular with the actresses than Massie? Her ears started ringing and her palms went clammy.

"Kirk Morrison told me your dad is building you a school."

"Oh, that." She exhaled and wiped her hands on her satin pj's. "Yeah, and it's going to be coed."

"Can I go?"

"Yup. But no shorts allowed," Massie teased.

"Who's gonna stop me?" He turned around and wiggled his butt for the girls.

Massie felt a tingle in the tiny space behind her belly button while everyone laughed with her boyfriend.

Feelings like these made her grateful there was a computer between them. She was terrified of another awkward is-he-about-to-make-a-move moment—like the one they had in Lake Placid before they kissed. The unpredictability of it all made Massie's internal organs pretzel. It was kind of like puking in that way; having the feeling, knowing it was about to happen, but not knowing exactly when. And Massie hated puking.

"Claire." Cam looked into the camera with his one blue eye and one green eye. "Is it true your brother felt up Abby Boyd?"

"*Ew*, no!" Claire turned red.

"So he wasn't lying." Josh pulled off his New York Yankees cap and whipped it onto the gray carpet. "That kid is incredible."

"She's not that hot in person, you know," Alicia chimed in, obviously jealous that Josh was jealous of Todd. "Her hair is super short now. She looks like—"

"Like what?" Kristen cocked her head.

"Forget it."

"Hey, Kristen." Derrington pushed the hair away from his eyes. "Did you hear we got a new soccer coach?"

"It's about time. Do you like him?"

"He's awesome. Yesterday during drills he made us—"

"Zzzzzzzz." Massie fake-snored.

"Hey!" Claire shouted. "Look." She pressed her finger against the monitor and Massie smacked it away.

"Don't touch the screen."

"But look." Kristen leaned into the computer and squinted. "It's Rupert Mann."

"'Ello, oym Rooopert Mannn." Josh attempted to impersonate the British director.

He got an I'm-so-embarrassed-for-you shove from Cam and a giggle from Alicia.

"Rupert? Where? Hide me!" Dylan shouted from the bathroom.

"He's on TV. Behind you!" Claire pointed. "What are you watching?"

"I dunno, one of those stupid Hollywood gossip shows," Derrington mumbled. "My sister was watching it."

"Yeah, right!" Josh punched Derrington on the arm.

"She was!" He returned the punch with his back to the camera, obviously trying to hide his guilty smile.

"Then why is your face purple?" Cam chuckled.

"It's *not*!" Derrington elbowed him. "Maybe if your eyes were the same color you'd know that."

Massie pressed her nose against the screen, ignoring their little brawl. "Channel seven! Quick!"

Everyone raced around the room looking for the remote except Claire. She sat patiently, obviously hoping to continue her conversation with Cam.

"We'll call you after the show," Massie announced.

"'Kay," the boys replied in a chorus of cracked voices.

"Cam, wait!" Claire shouted.

"E-mail him later." Massie clicked off the computer.

"Ehmagawd." Alicia threw herself onto Massie's fluffy white duvet. "There he is."

The other girls squeezed beside her. And Bean jumped straight onto Massie's lap.

"He still has my phone."

"Who cares?" Alicia kicked off her Steve Madden leopard slippers. "Your new Motorola Razr is cooler."

"I know, but I miss the purple rhinestones."

"Shhhh." Kristen lifted a finger to her lips. "We're missing the whole interview."

The girls focused on the TV.

"I love Ama-ri-cn cinema, Joanie, dawn't get me wrung." Rupert crossed his legs and rested a hand on his denim-clad kneecap. His blue Lacoste pique polo matched his eyes a little too well for the pairing to have been an accident, yet the cameraman seemed more interested in the pack of Big Red gum he was flipping between his fingers. "It's just that the actors in yoh country ah such divas. I find them very unpleasant to work with."

"Have you cast anyone to replace Hadley Durk?" Joanie pulled off her cat's-eye glasses and leaned forward on her stool. "I heard rumors about Tara LeWine." She quickly put the glasses back on, as if they doubled as a hearing aid.

"Right, well." He tapped his thigh with the Big Red. "Tah-ra would be fabulous if I had anotha twenty mil in my budget. But I'm afraid I dawn't."

The camera cut to a close-up shot of Joanie shaking her head sympathetically.

"So I'm gaaw-ing to try something utta-ly revolutionary."

"Don't tell me—a computer-generated actress?"

"Hah-dly." Rupert chuckled politely, then turned to the camera. He held Massie's cell phone in front of the lens.

"Ehmagawd!" the girls screamed.

"Apple-C," they screamed again.

"I want to meet the girl who owns this celly," he announced. "I want you and those little friends of yoz to audition f' Hadley's role. No mo' divas. I wohnt a real, down-t-uth girl this time."

"Ehmagawd!" the girls screamed even louder.

"Apple-C," they screamed again.

"Sounds exciting." Joanie clapped her manicured hands together. She looked into the camera. "More on this revolutionary approach to casting after the break."

Massie automatically hit mute when a commercial for toe-fungus cream appeared on her screen.

"Call the show!" Claire urged.

"Wait." Dylan ran out of the bathroom. "Call my mom. She'll have his number."

"I'm with Claire," Kristen said. "Call the show."

"Can everyone please calm down?" Massie got off the bed and paced. She needed to think about this. The last thing she wanted was for a famous director to think she was a desperate wannabe. At the same time she didn't want him to think she wasn't interest—

Hola . . . hola.

Hola . . . hola.

Alicia reached for her ringing phone.

"Hello?" When she heard the voice on the other end, she rolled her eyes and hit speaker.

". . . and since you ah the first name in the address book I fig'ad I'd staht with you."

"Oh, really?" Alicia shook her head in a what-an-idiot sort of way, then whispered, "Josh."

The girls covered their mouths and lowered their ears closer to the phone.

"Yes, so, uh, do you know where I can find ha?" he continued.

"Too late." Alicia tugged on one of her braids. "She just left with Orlando Bloom, *Josh!*" She hit end and the line went dead.

"His accent was pretty good." Kristen giggled.

"Puh-lease." Alicia rolled her eyes. "My mother is Spanish, remember? I think I can tell a European accent when I hear one."

Pick up the phone. . . . Pick up the phone. . . .

"That's me." Claire lifted the ringing Nokia to her ear. "Hello?"

"I bet that's him again." Alicia tried to look annoyed, but her toothy smile betrayed her. She was loving Josh's little flirtation.

"Hit speaker!" Massie ordered.

Claire covered the mouthpiece. "Don't have it."

Massie rolled her eyes.

The more Claire listened, the wider her mouth opened.

"Okay, uh, would you mind giving me your number and I'll call you back from a better phone? My battery is dying. I can't hear you." Claire paused. "Oh, that's right. Good point. Okay. 'Bye, Rupert."

"*What?*" Massie shrieked. "Was that really Rupert? How do you *know*?"

"He said to call your old phone and he'll answer."

"Ehmagawd." Kristen buried her face in her hands. "How ahb-vious is that?"

Massie's head began to throb. Why hadn't she thought of that? Was all this free time making her soft?

She pulled out her Razr and flipped it open. Her gold charm bracelet jiggled as she began dialing her old number.

Once it rang, she dove onto her bed and hit speaker.

"Hullo, Cleh?"

"Ehmagawd!" Massie mouthed as she slapped her mattress.

"Uh, yeah . . . I mean, I'm here. . . . I mean, yes . . . this is Claire." She fanned her cheeks.

"As I wuz saying, I'm looking for the gul who owns this phone, and yo name was second in her address book so—"

"Rupert? It's me, Massie. The owner." She grabbed a fistful of goose down and squeezed.

"Wonderful. This is Rupert Mann. And I am looking to do something totally new with this pick-cha."

"Uh-huh." Massie did her best to sound calm despite the fact that her friends were all on their backs, kicking their legs in the air. She felt like she was watching a synchronized swimming show on mute.

"I want to fly you and your friends out to L.A. next week on the studio's private jet so you can audition."

"*Private jet!*" Kristen's blue eyes were wide. "PRIVATE JET!"

"L.A.!" Alicia grabbed her and they hugged and bounced until Kristen fell off the bed and face-planted on Massie's floor.

"Is that them?" he asked politely.

"Um, yeah." Massie smacked her hand down on the bed, urging them to stay cool. "Sorry, Rupert, what were you saying?"

"The auditions ah on Monday. Then it's a three-week shoot in L.A. Is that going to be a problem with school?"

"Um, no. No problem at all. We'll get out of school for this." She kicked her bare feet in the air.

Everyone giggled.

"Yes, but fo three weeks?"

"Whatever it takes." Massie bit her bottom lip. "Our principal gives us time off when we get acting jobs."

Alicia gave her a thumbs-up.

"Oh." Rupert sounded disappointed. "So you have experience?"

"Oh yeah."

"Because I am after an unknown, so—"

"I mean, you don't count one day of extra work, do you?"

"Ha-dly." He chuckled.

"Then we're good."

The girls applauded silently.

"Oh, and one lawst thing—"

"Yup?"

"Dawn't bring the redhead."

Dylan gasped.

Massie looked at her and shrugged. "Why not?"

"She's the reason Hadley quit the pick-cha, and I dawn't need any bad ena-gy on my set."

"It was an accident!" Dylan burst into tears, then grabbed an unopened basket of sugar cookies and locked herself in the bathroom.

"Who was that?" Rupert asked.

"The redhead," Massie murmured.

"Tragic. How 'bout I give yo parents a buzz tomorrow and we'll fuhm up the travel?"

"Sounds good." Massie's knees were shaking. "You have the number."

"Actually, I don't."

"Oh." Massie giggled, then gave him her home number.

"See you in a few days, then." Rupert sounded like he was smiling.

"See you in a few days." Massie snapped her phone shut, then tossed it on her bed. "Ehmagawd! *We're going to be movie stars.*"

"Speak for yourself!" Dylan wailed from the bathroom.

But the girls were too excited to comfort Dylan. They

jumped up on the bed and screamed and hugged and bounced while Bean got tossed about like a kernel in an air popper.

"Wait." Massie stopped suddenly. "You realize only one of us is going to get the part."

"Point," Alicia panted.

And just like that, everyone stopped hugging.

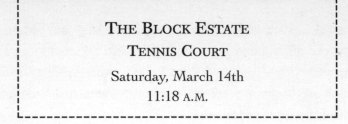

Claire shielded her eyes from the sun when she stepped into the Blocks' yard, almost spilling the two glasses of lemonade she was balancing on a silver tray. It was August-bright, and the temperature was hovering around seventy degrees. Everything smelled like a mix of fresh-cut grass and ice water. It was turn-over-a-new-leaf weather. It was first-love weather. It was I-feel-happy-for-no-reason weather. Still, Claire's cuticles were picked raw.

"Stop worrying." Massie took the tray from her, set it on the patio table, then wiped the lenses of her Oliver Peoples aviators. "March is never this warm. It's a sign." She slid on her glasses and picked up the tray.

"What kind of sign?"

"A sign we were meant to be in Hollywood." She tilted her face toward the bright sun. "It's like this all the time there." Massie rolled up the sleeves of the gray jersey dress she'd haphazardly thrown over a pair of skinny jeans. Claire was still in her Powerpuff Girls pj's from the night before.

"What if our parents say no?" Claire couldn't imagine her mom and dad letting her jet off to California when *Cam's* house—which was around the corner—had been declared off-limits.

"That's why we're going to their tennis game." Massie stopped walking and lowered her voice.

For a few seconds, the only sounds were birds and the *pop . . . pop . . . pop* of the ball getting whacked from one side of the court to the other.

Massie pulled off her glasses. "Remember, this is all about kissing massive amounts of butt."

Claire nodded once for "got it."

"Don't let them know we want something. They have to think we're being helpful and sweet because we're helpful and sweet. Then when Rupert calls, they'll flash back to our ah-dorable helpfulness and they'll say yes."

"'Kay."

"Now, let's take a moment and pray for our auditions."

Massie lowered her head.

"Should we pray Alicia and Kristen get permission too?" Claire asked.

"Probably not."

They closed their eyes.

"Switch!" William Block hollered. He wiped his head with a towel as he and Kendra changed sides with Judi and Jay Lyons. He was in pretty good shape for a dad. Muscular legs, toned arms, and a slight belly. Nothing like Jay, who was panting and sweating as if he'd been chasing a Ben and Jerry's delivery truck.

"Now!" Massie whispered.

"Lemonade!" Claire practically sang the word. "Fresh lemonade here."

"Come and get it!"

Todd jogged over to the gate. "Awesome!" He crammed a ball into the pocket of his shorts and reached for an icy glass.

"It's not for you." Claire pulled the tray away. "It's for Mom and Dad."

"No way," Todd whined. "I got here first. I'm working this game."

"Forget it." Massie pushed past him. "We have serious ass-kissing to do."

"I ran off to New York, remember?" He flipped the collar on his polo shirt. "I'm looking at a year with no video games, maybe two."

"Lemonade!" Massie shouted.

"Balls!" Todd shouted louder.

"LEMONADE!" Claire yelled.

"BALLS!"

"Okay, okay." William waved his white towel as a show of surrender. "Let's take five."

"Thank heavens," Judi huffed. Her chestnut-brown bangs were matted to her forehead. "I didn't realize I was in such bad shape."

"I'm telling you, dear." Kendra smoothed her pleated skirt. "Pilates can fix all that." She poked Judi's back fat with the head of her racket.

Judi's smile faded.

"You are a couple of angels." Jay lifted a glass off Claire's tray and finished it in one gulp. "Ahhhhhhh."

"There's more in the house if you want us to get it." Massie tilted her head and smiled.

"Or we can make sandwiches," Claire offered. "I bet you're hungry."

"Yeah, sandwiches," Todd urged the parents. "Wouldn't that be great, Dad?"

Claire shot him a dirty look.

"It would, son." Jay put his arm around Todd. "I'll take turkey on a roll with cheese, mayo, lettuce, and a pickle on the side."

"Sounds good." William licked his lips. "But hold the mayo on mine, add mustard, and throw in an extra pickle."

Kendra twisted the diamond stud in her ear. "I'll have mine on a whole-wheat wrap. Mustard only."

"I'll have the same as Kendra." Judi grinned.

"And I'll have what Dad is having." Todd grinned. "With chips."

"Chips sound great, son." Jay mussed his hair. "Make that two chips."

"Uh," Massie dug her nails into Claire's wrist. "Can I speak to you for a minute?"

"Sure." Claire held up a finger as Massie dragged her onto the lawn. "We'll be back in one minute to take your drink orders."

"Are you insane?" Massie whisper-shouted once they were alone.

"What are you so mad about?" Claire shook her wrist free. "They're loving us right now."

"They were loving us with the lemonade. Why did you have to get all Subway on them?"

"I thought that's what you wanted!"

"Uh, I don't remember saying, 'Hey, let's spend the day making sandwiches for your family.'"

"Your parents want them too!" Claire heard her voice begin to shake.

"Well, then, I hope you know how to cook." Massie marched over to the court. She stopped a few feet short of the gate, then exhaled slowly. Her next inhalation brought forth a pleasant flight-attendant smile that practically connected the corners of her mouth to the bottom of her sunglasses. "We'll be right back with lunch," she cooed.

Claire spent the next half hour slicing, spreading, and Saran-ing while Massie filed her toenails.

"All done." Claire screwed the top on the jar of mayo and wiped down the cutting board. She wrapped her arms around all five sandwiches and both bags of chips. "Let's go."

"Wait!" Massie flip-flopped into the pantry and pulled out a picnic basket. "Put them in here. Presentation is everything."

Claire unloaded the sandwiches, then reached for the handle.

"That's okay." Massie's expression was kind, almost caring. "You made them; the least I can do is carry them outside."

"Maybe we should both carry them." Claire could hear her heart beating inside her chest. "That way they'll know they came from both of us."

"Puh-lease." Massie rolled her eyes and pushed through the side door, swinging the goods. "You've done so much already. Relax."

During their silent walk back to the courts, Claire opened and closed her fists, trying to release the anger that was welling up in her fingertips. Was this her fault for being such a pushover? Or Massie's for being so pushy?

"Your lunch is here!" Massie unpacked the basket on the bench by the net.

No one hesitated to dig in.

"These are great, love." Kendra dabbed the corner of her lip with a cloth napkin.

"Thanks, Mom." Massie beamed.

"You just sounded British," William teased.

Claire and Massie exchanged a glance.

"I did, didn't I?" Kendra covered her mouth while she chewed.

"Speaking of British . . ." Judi swallowed. "Some strange British man called the house this morning."

"He called us too!" Kendra crossed her toned legs.

"What did you do?" Massie asked. "Did you talk to him?"

"I hope you hung up." William balled his Saran wrap and tossed it in the trash. "I am so incredibly sick of those tele-marketers."

"Of course I did."

"Good for you." Jay batted the crumbs out of his beard. "If I want something, I'll buy it myself, thank you."

"I agree." Judi rested her arm on her husband's shoulder.

"Wait, Mom." Claire's armpits started to sweat. "You hung up?"

"I did." Judi nodded, obviously proud of her decision.

Massie crossed her leg and began shaking her foot. "Uh, I think we may know who that was."

"Yeah, we would have told you but we didn't think he'd call so early," Claire added.

The parents stared, all looking very concerned, waiting for them to continue.

"His name is Rupert Mann and he's a big Hollywood director," Massie began.

"Wait, I thought he was British." William rubbed his sunburned head.

"He is, Dad, but he works in Hollywood."

"Ohhh, silly me." He knocked his bald spot. "Sorry. Go on."

Massie continued, "So anyway, he wants us to audition for his new movie and—"

"And we're flying to Los Angeles first thing Monday morning on the studio's private jet, right?" Judi snickered.

"We are?" Todd jumped up and down. Three fluorescent yellow balls fell out of his pocket and rolled onto the court.

"Uh, close." Claire looked at Massie, wondering how mothers always managed to guess right.

"No, not kind of." Kendra grinned. "Definitely."

"*Huh?*" The bottoms of Claire's feet tingled. "What do you mean?"

"I mean we spoke to Rupert this morning," Kendra continued. "We told him it was okay."

"Wait," Massie asked, confused. "You said yes?"

Judi squealed with delight. "Surprise!"

"Ehmagawd!" Massie and Claire yelled, then grabbed each other's shoulders and began jumping.

"On two conditions." Kendra's voice grew stern.

They immediately stopped moving, their smiles fading fast.

"What?" Massie put a hand on her hip.

"Rupert offered to hire an on-set tutor for whoever gets the part. And if that person gets a single grade below an A, she is off the movie."

"But that's not—"

"Don't forget, you have been expelled." Kendra wagged an index finger in her daughter's face. "This tutor will help you keep up with your old classmates. She might even save you from having to repeat the seventh grade."

"What about the person who *doesn't* get the part?" Claire yanked a hangnail off her thumb, then clenched her fist against the pain.

"Rupert will send a tutor for the girls who don't get the part too—a consolation prize, as he put it." Judi lifted her thin eyebrows as if to say, *Can you believe how lucky we got?*

"Some prize," Massie said under her breath.

"This is awesome!" Claire clapped her hands. "Now I'll only have to spend one year at ADD instead of two."

Massie rolled her eyes, then turned to her mother. "What was the second condition?"

"Your mother and I get to chaperone," Judi gushed.

"So we can go?" Massie widened her amber eyes.

"We talked about it and agreed that this is a once-in-a-lifetime opportunity," William said.

"You too?" Claire asked her father.

Jay nodded.

Claire threw her arms around her father's neck.

"Besides, if OCD doesn't let you back in, you'll need the work," he added.

"But remember, nothing below an A," William reminded them.

"Deal." Massie shook her father's hand. After a quick moment, her expression changed from one of elation to one of suspicion. She pulled off her sunglasses and glared at her parents. "So the lemonade and the sandwiches—"

"Not necessary." William chuckled.

"Delicious." Jay mussed Claire's hair. "But not necessary."

"Dad, can I go too?" Todd hopped into his father's lap and kissed his cheek.

"Yup."

"Yeahhhhhh!" Todd jumped down and ran around the court.

"Dad!" Claire was about to explain that Todd would embarrass her and totally ruin her chances of getting any part, but saw the playful flicker behind her father's eyes and knew she wouldn't have to.

"I'm going to Hollywood. I'm going to Hollywood," Todd sang.

"In 2010!" Jay shouted. "When you're not grounded."

Todd stopped running, then slowly began gathering tennis balls. One by one, he whipped them over the fence.

"I quit!" he shouted, and took off for the guesthouse.

"I'd ask if anyone wants to play one last game, but we're out of balls." William stood.

"That's okay." Kendra zipped a black padded cover around her tennis racket. "We have to start packing. We leave in less than two days."

"Claire, come up to my room and we'll call Alicia and Kristen," Massie suggested.

"'Kay," Claire said. But all she really wanted to do was hop on her bike and ride to Cam's house. They could sit on the hood of his brother's Mustang and talk about how much they were going to miss each other while Claire sniffed his neck. If her allowance hadn't been suspended, she would have bought a bottle of Drakkar Noir and sprayed it on her pillow, just so she could spend all night breathing the manly blend of lavender, citrus, spicy berries, and sandalwood that was Cam Fisher.

"You know, if I get this part, I won't see Cam for three more weeks." She stomped up the steps behind Massie. "That will make it twenty-nine days total. What if he meets someone else?"

"Puh-lease. You have nothing to worry about." Massie placed her hand on Claire's shoulder. "Cam ah-dores you."

Claire's insides flooded with warmth while she considered this.

"And besides." Massie continued up the stairs. "You won't get the part."

Claire lay in bed outlining the glittery stars on her comforter with her throbbing index finger. How could she go to Hollywood with swollen, ripped-up cuticles? Why not tattoo NERVOUS WRECK across her forehead instead? It would be a lot less hideous.

But no matter how repulsive her nails were, she couldn't stop picking. She'd think about Cam meeting another girl and pick. Or imagine auditioning for Rupert. And pick. Or remember she was competing against Massie for the role. Pick. Or fear going to ADD. Pick. Where she'd be forced to buy back her stolen lunch for a hundred dollars. Pick. Or—

Click.

Finally! The sound she'd been waiting for. Her parents had shut their bedroom door. The coast was clear.

Claire pulled her comforter over her head and switched on the PowerBook G4 laptop Massie had loaned her. The illuminated computer screen filled her cotton fortress with a blue glow and her heart with what felt like helium.

"Yes!" There was a green dot beside FISHER2, Cam's IM screen name. He was waiting for her.

Claire hit the keys as softly and quietly as she could, hoping the comforter would muffle the tapping that could betray her to her parents at any time. If they caught her online after taking away her computer, L.A. would be out of the question.

CLAIREBEAR: Sorry. ☹ Parents just went 2 sleep.
FISHER2: s'okay.
CLAIREBEAR: They said ok to LA. Can U believe?
FISHER2: !! U X-ited?
CLAIREBEAR: Nervous.

Claire stared at the blinking cursor until it blurred. Cam wasn't responding. Was he mad she was leaving? Did he want to break up with her? Was he IM-ing someone else at the same time? Someone with nice nails?

CLAIREBEAR: Still there?
FISHER2: Yeah. Just bummed.
CLAIREBEAR: ??
FISHER2: miss u.

Claire wanted to dive into the screen and grab him. She wanted to inhale his grape-bubble-gum breath and draw in the ocean smell of his beat-up leather jacket. If only she could gaze into his blue eye and then his green eye, touch his warm cheek, and lip-kiss him for a full minute. Then, when the minute was up, she'd crawl back into the computer and write up every detail so she could relive it ten times a day while she was gone.

CLAIREBEAR: Miss U 2. I'll take tons of pictures and call you every day. Promise.
FISHER2: Don't fall in love with any movie stars.
CLAIREBEAR: Don't fall in love with anyone.
FISHER2: Too late. ☺

Claire opened her mouth and silent-screamed—or as silently as someone *whose boyfriend just said, "I love you"* possibly could.

The kitten heels on Massie's metallic slides echoed against the metal steps as she climbed toward the belly of the Gelding 7 jet.

"Girls, hurry up!" Judi Lyons poked her head out the plane's doorway and lifted a bottle of Perrier to her thin lips. "Claire, it's nicer than the hotel we stayed in when our roof was leaking."

"Really?" Claire squeezed past Massie and hurried up the narrow steps. She was wearing what looked like a pair of green doctor's scrubs, a faded yellow long-sleeved tee, and her black-and-white Keds, even though they didn't match.

"No way!" she shouted when she climbed aboard. "You guys *have* to see this!"

"Lame," Massie muttered to Alicia, who was a few steps behind her. "Why do the Lyonses always act so *impressed* with everything? It makes them sound so un-rich."

"Point," Alicia panted.

She was dressed in the exact same wide-leg James Perse lounge pants as Massie, only hers were navy and Massie's were olive. On top they wore striped C&C shirts over long white beaters. These were their plane outfits. Comfortable, yet cute enough to wear to the nearest department store should they lose their luggage.

"Mmmmm." Alicia inhaled deeply once they boarded. "Warm cinnamon buns."

Massie's mouth watered. The Gelding 7 didn't have that dusty-carpet smell other airplanes had. And the air didn't feel thick with the flu virus and coffee breath. If Glossip Girl made a Gelding 7 flavor, it would smell like the inside of a baker's oven: warm, fresh, and sweet.

"Welcome." A sunny blond flight attendant smiled as she handed each of the girls a champagne flute filled with sparkling lemon water and a plate of bite-size sandwich wraps that had been rolled up to look like sushi. PB&J, tuna, and cheese were among the assortment.

"Kristen would have loved this." Alicia ran her fingers along the textured gold wallpaper. Every time she came to a window, she pinched the velvet curtains, then rubbed them between her fingers, as if she suspected they might be polyester in disguise. But they weren't. "I can't believe she wasn't allowed to come."

"Mrs. Gregory can be such a female dog," Massie said to what looked like an original Matisse, one of the many colorful paintings in the cabin.

"I bet she's upset no one asked *her* to be in a movie," Alicia said.

"If they did, it would be called *Dial J for Jealous*."

"Nice." Alicia high-fived her.

"Massie, that's not fair." Kendra pulled the plastic off

her complimentary beige cashmere slippers and slid them onto her manicured feet. "She has every reason to punish Kristen."

And we have every reason to think she's a female dog, Massie thought. But all she said was, "You're right. Sorry." She had to keep up the good-girl act, at least until the auditions were over, just in case her mother decided to get all Gregory on her.

A light flashed in the back of the cabin.

"What was that?" Judi asked from the leather couch.

"Me!" shouted Claire. "I was taking a picture for Cam."

As far as Massie could see, the only thing back there was the bathroom. "Of what?"

"Come see."

Alicia and Massie hurried past ten reclining seats, each with its own TV, DVD player, and PSP system.

"It's a magic glass wall." Claire knocked it with her knuckle. "Go in the bathroom, I'll show you."

Massie stepped inside and looked out at Claire and Alicia. "So what's the big deal?"

"Can you see us?" Claire was waving.

"Yeah. Can you see me?" Massie pressed her face against the glass. But no one cracked a smile.

"*No!*" Claire and Alicia said together.

"Apple-C!" they shouted and punched each other's arms.

"Can you see me now?" Massie pressed her butt against the glass.

"No." Claire giggled. "That's the whole point—you can see out, but no one can see in. How cool is that?"

"It's called a tinted window, Kuh-laire." Massie opened the door. "Every limo in the world has them."

"But bathrooms don't." Claire's smile waned. "And look." She raced over to the control panel next to the shiny red toilet. "It has a seat warmer, a back massager, an overhead light for reading, and two different fountains that shoot water into your—"

"Ew." Massie jumped back. "Why?"

"So you don't get their fancy t.p. dirty." Alicia waved a roll of black toilet paper. The gold Gelding Studios pony was embossed on every sheet.

"Gimme that." Massie stuffed the roll in her Louis Vuitton Batignolles bag. "Kristen and Dylan won't believe it."

"How many limos have all this?"

Massie ignored Claire to answer her ringing phone.

Yap-yap-yap . . .

Yap-yap-yap . . .

A close-up of Dylan's green eye flashed on her screen. She pressed speaker.

"Hello?"

"I can't believe I'm not with you guys." Dylan sniffled.

"I know. We miss you."

"We already got you a present!" Alicia beamed.

"And we'll iSight you with the gossip every night," Massie added.

"Pinky-swear?" Dylan sniffled again.

"Pinky-swear." Massie held up her pinky, forgetting that Dylan couldn't see it. "Remember, keep an eye on Derrington."

"And Cam!" Claire added.

"And Josh," Alicia said.

"Make sure Kristen doesn't use the whole soccer thing as an excuse to flirt with them," Massie reminded her.

"'Kay." Dylan blew her nose.

"Ladies, please take your seats and prepare for takeoff," a friendly female voice said over the intercom.

"Ehmagawd! We're *leaving*!" Massie shrieked.

"Wait," Dylan pleaded.

"Call you later." Massie hung up.

The girls grabbed three seats in the back, as far away from their mothers as possible. While the plane taxied, they unzipped their complimentary Coach makeup bags and sampled the different moisturizers and lip balms inside. Claire wore the pink satin eye mask as a bracelet and Alicia spritzed her cheeks with peppermint-scented face mist.

"Hollywood rules!" Massie sighed dreamily as she wrapped a navy cashmere blanket around her shoulders and fluffed her down-filled pillow.

The Gelding 7 began rolling down the runway, slow at first, then faster. The nose lifted, and within seconds they were flying over New York City, heading straight for the stars.

WELCOME TO LOS ANGELES! was the first thing Claire saw when Avery R., the eager bellboy, clicked open the door to their hotel suite. It was written with Reese's Pieces on a gigantic chocolate chip cookie and displayed in the vestibule on a round mirrored table next to a tall vase of sunflowers.

"It was delivered an hour ago," explained Avery R. as he wheeled a gold cart—loaded with six Louis Vuitton suitcases and one red canvas hockey bag that had "Todd is God" scribbled across the top—into the bedroom.

"Who's it from?" Alicia asked as she spritzed her cheeks with Evian spray mist.

"Lemme check." Claire kicked off her Keds, anxious to sink her bare feet into the freshly vacuumed cream-colored rug. Then she opened the card and read, "To my future starlet. Hollywood awaits you! Best, Rupert. P.S. Enjoy this cookie now. It will be your last."

Claire reached inside the side pocket of her scrubs and wrapped her hand around a sweaty cellophane bulge. It contained five gummy worms, the last of her stash from Cam. Her plan was to save them for moments of extreme loneliness, the times she missed him most. She'd already eaten one during takeoff.

Massie snatched the card out of Claire's hand and dropped it in her bag. "I'm going to scan it for our newsletter." She pinched a Reese's Piece off the cookie and popped it in her mouth. "We better freshen up. Rupert's assistant, Emma, is picking us up in the lobby in half an hour."

Claire photographed every inch of the suite, which looked more like the inside of a Tiffany box than a hotel room. The walls were painted robin's-egg blue, and the circular couch in the middle of the grand living area was covered in white satin. The coffee table was made of mirrors and matched the two diamond-shaped end tables, reminding Claire of Kendra's "Sunday" earrings.

A massive floor-to-ceiling window, to the right of the couch, gave them a clear view of the famous Hollywood sign.

"I trust everything is to your liking?" Avery R. emerged from the bedroom with an empty cart. He blotted his forehead with a hanky, then stuffed it in the lapel pocket of his red blazer.

"It's awesome." Claire ran her fingers along the sleek computer that sat on the mirrored desk by the balcony. She slid open one of the drawers, expecting to find a Bible. Instead, she came across a special-edition Montblanc pen made of Baccarat crystal, and several notebooks with mirrored covers.

"It's fine." Massie yawned, as if describing a pullout bed that would simply have to do.

"Yeah, it's cute." Alicia parroted Massie's blasé tone.

"Very good." Avery R. smiled, his teeth looking twenty years younger and brighter than the rest of him. He turned to Claire. "Let me show you how to work the controls."

"Cool." Claire followed Avery to the entertainment center while Massie and Alicia took off in search of their bags.

"We pride ourselves on being completely wireless." He tapped the mirrored console below the fifty-inch flat-screen TV. Stacks of current fashion magazines and newspapers were fanned across the top. Below them were a DVD player, a CD player, and an iPod dock. To the right, by the window, was a cabinet with a keyhole, which Claire assumed was the minibar, plus a popcorn maker and a Starbucks espresso machine. And not a single wire anywhere.

"You can control the entire suite with this." Avery R. held up an egg-shaped remote, dotted with flat, backlit buttons that said things like TV, AIR-CONDITIONING, WINDOW SHADES, COFFEEMAKER, POPCORN POPPER, and BUBBLE BATH. "If you want something done, press the button." He handed it to Claire.

"No way!" She pressed bubble bath and instantly heard the thundering sound of rushing water.

"Whoa!" Alicia called from the bathroom. "This tub just read my mind."

"Thanks, Avery R." Massie appeared, her dark brown extensions twisted and pinned to the top of her head. "We have to get ready now." She slapped a twenty-dollar bill in his chalky palm.

"Thanks." His tired eyes sprang to life. "Your mothers are right next door, but if you need anything, please call me."

"Will do." Massie padded off to the bedroom.

Claire broke into a full sprint and ran past her. "This place is huge!" She pushed open the French doors, took four huge strides, then dove onto the satin-cloaked California king bed, still holding the egg. "This mattress is the size of my entire room back home."

"You better change out of those scrubs." Massie sat on the clear Lucite stool in front of the vanity and unzipped her Prada makeup bag. "Or you may end up with a part on *Grey's Anatomy* by accident."

Claire skipped into the walk-in closet. She stepped over the minefield of clothes, shoes, boots, hair dryers, and jewelry boxes that were hemorrhaging from the Louis Vuitton suitcases. Finally she found her hockey bag stuffed in the corner between an ironing board and a laundry hamper.

"Ew!" Claire squealed. While she was fishing around for her audition outfit, her hand landed on a pair of Todd's Harry Potter briefs. Either they'd gotten mixed up in her laundry, or her brother hadn't bothered to clean his bag since hockey camp. She quickly pulled out her pink Gap tee and cutoff Levi's and zipped it back up.

"I think I grew on the flight," she told her reflection as she lodged Cam's bag of gummies in her back pocket.

"The only thing that grew is the hair on your legs." Massie slammed her Secret deodorant down on the makeup vanity. "I can see it from here." She marched across the bedroom toward the closet.

Alicia giggled. "Me too!" she called from the tub.

Claire brushed her hand along her calf. There was definitely hair there, but her mother always said it was blond and that no one could see it. "How bad is it? Out of ten. Ten being 'early man.'"

"Six." Massie hooked the back seam on her pants, liberating them from her butt crack.

Claire snickered. It didn't surprise her that Massie had bought the same super-straight velvet pants Abby had worn on *The Daily Grind*. But she was shocked she'd chosen to debut them in seventy-six-degree weather.

"Step aside." Massie waved Claire off like a stinky fart, then tilted the floor-length mirror. "Now look. Still think you grew?"

"Oh," Claire said to her five-foot-three frame. "That's more like it."

"Clothes stores and five-star hotels use fun-house mirrors to trick stupid people into thinking they're suddenly tall and thin. You know, so they'll spend more money." She twisted her charm bracelet.

Claire's cheeks burned. "So you think I'm *stupid*?"

Massie triple-tapped her on the head and walked away.

"Did anyone happen to notice the ah-mazing products in the bathroom? It's better than Bendel's in there." Alicia emerged, towel-drying her thick dark hair, her boobs jiggling inside the waffled cotton Le Baccarat robe.

"Why aren't you dressed yet?" Massie snapped. "Emma is picking us up at eleven thirty."

"I have fifteen minutes." Alicia tossed her wet towel on the bed.

"This goes in the hamper." Massie slid a pink-satin-covered hanger under the wet towel and flipped it onto the floor.

Alicia picked the egg off the duvet and pressed radio. An old Kanye West song blasted through the speakers.

Claire danced her way into the bathroom, finally able to pee now that Alicia was gone. Red petals that had once dusted the floor were now wet and stuck to the marble thanks to Alicia's watery footprints. The deep tub gurgled as the bubbles drained out, and the doors of the shower were covered in steam. Above the two clear sinks was a long, mirrored cabinet. Claire slid it open and was over-whelmed by the heady aroma of plant extracts. The top shelf was filled with Bumble & Bumble hair products; the second with lotions and creams from Clarins, Kiehl's, and Philosophy; the third with miniature perfume samples and tiny bottles of Essie nail polish; and the fourth with Aveda soaps and oils.

"Ready!" Alicia shouted.

Claire grabbed a small green bar of soap, shoved it in her back pocket, and clicked off the light.

Alicia was twisting her hair into a chignon when Claire stepped out of the bathroom. Her I HEART NY tank top was cinched with a silver braided belt and covered with a shrunken white blazer. A black peasant skirt and metallic ballet slippers gave her a city-meets-country look that Rupert would probably love.

Then there was Massie. Usually she'd be classified as "actress beautiful," but her new long hair elevated her status to "model beautiful." She was wearing an ivory silk halter, a tangle of charm necklaces, and Abby's black velvet pants.

Next to Massie and Alicia, Claire felt like a sloppy first grader, more *Sesame Street* than sexy. Cam was the only one who liked her super short bangs, and it had been days since she'd seen him.

"Let's go!" Massie dabbed her wrists with Chanel No. 5, grabbed the key card, and marched out of the room. Alicia hooked a red hobo bag over her shoulder and followed. Claire slipped on her Hadley-approved Keds, snapped off a chunk of cookie, shoved it in her mouth, and closed the door behind her.

The elevator ride from the twenty-fifth floor to the lobby gave Claire enough time to hate her hair, detest her bloody cuticles, and abhor the dusting of hair on her thighs. What had made her think she could star in a movie? Having the lead in a few school plays back in Florida hardly qualified her as an actress. Massie and Alicia had even less experience, but they were Massie and Alicia. What else did they need?

Claire slid her fingers into the back pocket of her tight cutoffs and wrapped her hand around the miniature Aveda beauty bar. Then, as if wiping away a loose booger, she brushed the soap past her nostril and inhaled deeply. The combination of mint and flowers instantly calmed her nerves.

When the elevator doors opened, Massie lifted her chin and stepped into the bustling lobby.

"Oh, they look so glamorous, don't they, Kendra?" shrieked Judi.

Everyone turned to see who she was talking about.

"Puh-lease tell your mother to chill." Massie practically spat the words.

"Girls, go stand by that fountain so I can take a picture." Judi lifted a disposable camera out of a plastic Le Baccarat bag, normally used for trash, and waved it around. "Your grandparents will be so excited to see—"

"Look, that must be Emma." Massie grabbed Claire and Alicia and dragged them toward the dimly lit lounge.

Claire glanced back at her mother and flashed an I'd-love-to-stay-but-I'm-being-taken-against-my-will look, hoping it would explain the lost photo op.

Emma was in an oversize wing chair, talking on her cell. Just as she'd said she would be, she was dressed in a white linen pantsuit. "Royt, then, sounds good," her voice boomed in a thick British accent. "The girls ah he-ah. Gohdda jump." She dropped the phone into her blazer pocket.

Even though she was from England, Emma reminded Claire of the students at University of Central Florida. She had straight blond hair and wispy bangs. Her hazel eyes were lined with blue kohl and her lipstick was pink. Her B-cups weren't enhanced, her nose had a small bump, and her hand-bag didn't resemble luggage. Claire liked her immediately.

"Sorry 'bout that." She sighed. "The press has been up me bum all moh-ning. The-hh desperate to find out who will be replacing Hadley."

"Aren't we all." Alicia clutched her stomach.

Claire nodded.

"Look no further." Massie curtsied.

Emma threw her head back and laughed.

Alicia rolled her eyes.

Claire sighed, letting Alicia know that Massie's blatant campaigning annoyed her too.

"Emma, I'd like you to meet my manager." Massie waved her mother over. Judi followed.

"Pleasure to meet you." Kendra offered her right hand. A landslide of diamond tennis bracelets fell toward her bony wrist.

"And this is my mom." Claire pulled Judi into the circle.

"We are so excited to be here. Thanks for having us," Judi gushed, as if Emma had invited them to stay in her house and offered up her bed.

"So, are we ready?" Massie interrupted. "We don't want to keep Rupert waiting."

"I like that." Emma smiled. "A true professional."

"I try."

Claire wondered if she should bother auditioning. If she left now, she could be back under her covers IM'ing Cam before dinner.

"So, what do the chaperones do while the girls are auditioning?" Kendra slid her oversize Chanel sunglasses over her eyes.

"Ru-puhht would prefeh it if you stayed back heh. You know, so the guhls can really focus."

Claire felt a pinch of guilt because her mom had been excited to see Gelding Studios. But mostly she was relieved. When it came to getting crushed by Massie Block and Alicia Rivera, the fewer witnesses, the better.

"Hmmm." Kendra turned to Judi. "Have you ever been to Rodeo Drive?"

Judi adjusted her yellow visor. "No."

"You'll love it. It's like Fifth Avenue without the fur." Kendra winked at Massie.

"Ready, then?" Emma signaled her driver, who pulled up to the curb in a white Escalade.

"Ready," they all said at once.

"Apple-C!"

"Good luck, girls!" Kendra and Judi doled out a round of hugs, then stepped into a taxi by the valet stand. They blew air kisses out the window as they pulled onto Santa Monica Boulevard.

The girls spread out in the back of the spacious Escalade, and Emma sat up front with the driver, making phone calls.

Massie searched the satellite radio for a good pop station, while Alicia and Claire scoured the fridge. "Look at all this." Alicia snapped pictures of the soda, cookies, and mini-sandwiches with her Motorola Pebl, then e-mailed them to Dylan and Kristen.

"What are these?" Claire wiggled a bright red piece of licorice in Alicia's face, then took a bite.

Massie cranked up a dance-remix version of Christina Aguilera's old song "Beautiful."

"They're called Red Vines," Alicia shouted over the speedy electronica. "They're like the California version of Twizzlers."

"Much chewier, stickier, and more cherryish." Claire held out the plastic bag. "Want one?"

Alicia turned away in disgust.

"*I am beautiful, no matter what they say,*" Massie bellowed as she rolled down the windows. A rush of sun-kissed air blew through the SUV. For the first time in months, Claire felt warm.

Iambeautifulnomatterwhattheysay
Wordswon'tbringmedown. . . .

They sang as fast as they could, laughing as they tried to keep up with the accelerated pace of the remix.

Claire held her mouth open, trying to swallow as much of Los Angeles as she could. The blue ocean was on her left, and straight ahead a ridge of jagged mountains kissed the horizon. Claire thought of Orlando when they passed a row of tall palm trees and thought of Cam when they passed everything else. She reached into her back pocket, pulled out a yellow gummy worm, and gently placed it on her tongue.

Massie jumped to lower the radio and answered her barking phone. "Hey, Kristen. What's up? I'm putting you on speaker, 'kay?"

A chorus of sobs and sniffles filled the Escalade.

"Is Dylan there too?" Massie asked.

"Yessss," Dylan bawled.

"Why are you guys crying?" asked Claire. "Did something happen with the board? Do I have to go to ADD? Please don't say I have to go to ADD."

"We don't." Kristen sniffed.

"Then what is it?" Massie was annoyed.

"Why did Alicia send us those pictures?" Dylan blew her nose.

"I wanted you to see all of the food they have for us." Alicia grinned. "Isn't it great?"

"Were you *trying* to make us feel like LBRs?" Kristen snapped.

"Puh-lease." Alicia leaned closer to the phone. "I sent them so you could feel like you were here."

Kristen blew her nose.

"Do you miss us?" Dylan asked.

"Given." Alicia rolled her eyes.

"Do you think they've spoken to the boys yet?" Claire whispered.

"What?" Kristen barked. "Why are you whispering?"

"Sorry." Claire tugged on her short bangs. "I just wanted to know if you spoke to Cam yet."

"Or Josh?"

Claire glanced at Massie, expecting her to ask about Derrington, but she didn't. *How* did she have the willpower to act like she didn't care about him? Sometimes Claire wished she could act cool and aloof like Massie, even though it didn't seem like much fun.

"We'll see them tonight." Kristen perked up. "We're gonna dress up in hats and glasses and sneak into their soccer practice."

"Tell Cam I've been trying to call him but the time difference keeps messing things up." Claire's throat tightened when she said his name. She reached for a gummy worm but opted for the soap instead.

"I can't believe one of you will be in *Dial L for Loser*," Dylan whined. "It's so not fair."

"Weh hea," Emma announced while she waited for the driver to open her door.

"Ehmagawd," Massie gasped. "Gotta jump." She snapped her Razr shut.

"Who's ready to be a star?" Emma asked with a wink and a nod.

"Me!" Claire shouted.

But Massie and Alicia shouted louder and drowned her out.

The tall gates that separated Gelding Studios from the rest of the world parted as the Escalade rolled on in to what *Entertainment Weekly* coined "a billion-dollar playground for movie maniacs." Claire moaned.

"I should have shaved!" She stroked her shin. "It looks like I'm wearing yellow fleece tights."

"You could always audition for Big Bird's stand-in," Massie offered while finger-combing her extensions.

"Point." Alicia rubbed a dot of rosy tint on each of her cheeks.

Claire crossed her legs and turned toward the window.

A row of palm trees lined the center of Easy Street, the main roadway that led to different soundstages and sets on the lot. And gigantic movie posters of the studio's block-busters towered above them like Manhattan skyscrapers.

Emma tapped on her window. "On the right, heh, you'll see Horr-ah Road. All the scary movies ah shot theh. The house from *Blood Bahth* is a little ways in, and behind it is the black pond from *Snake Lake*."

Claire stuck her camera out the window and took a picture of the narrow wooden house that was surrounded by tombstones and fallen branches. It looked just like the poster in Cam's bedroom, minus the blood gushing from the windows.

"I slept in my parents' bed for a week after I saw that movie."

Massie and Alicia giggled.

"Same," Emma joked.

A golf cart filled with three astronauts zoomed past them and turned down Milky Way.

Massie gasped. "Ehmagawd, were those—"

"Yup." Emma nodded. "Those were the stahs of *T-Minus 3*. They built a huge moon set and, get this, a zero-gravity chamber." She faced them and lowered her voice. "I heard two of the stahs, Jayne Sauceland and Perry Most, were caught naked in theh last Friday night. The machine was tuhned up too high and instead of floating they weh plastehd to the wall and their bottoms were mashed up against the windows."

The girls burst out laughing.

The Escalade made a left down a nameless street that had a quaint sign that said WELCOME TO LAKEVIEW sticking out of a manicured hill.

"Here we ah," Emma announced.

Suddenly, as if transported by time machine, they were coasting down a winding neighborhood road. Each house had a landscaped front yard and a driveway with a basketball hoop, a hockey net, or a minivan blocking the garage. It could have easily passed for a normal suburban community if it weren't for the cranes and lights above every home.

"This is the make-believe town where *Dial L* is set." Emma unplugged her phone from the car charger and dropped in it her blazer pocket. "It's called Lakeview."

The Escalade turned into a crowded parking lot loaded with golf carts, utility trucks, snack-mobiles, and three long trailers. Straight ahead was a low, windowless football-field-size monstrosity of a building.

"This is Lakeview Middle School," Emma announced.

The driver turned off the car.

"Ew!" Alicia squealed. "This is even worse than ADD."

Claire's stomach clenched.

"The set is inside." Emma smiled as though she had built it herself. "It's really quite lovely."

Pick up your phone. . . . Pick up your phone. . . .

Claire pulled her Nokia out of her orange Kipling Fresh clutch. Her hands shook as she checked the display.

"Oh, hey, Layne." She groaned, unable to hide the fact that she had been hoping for Cam.

"Did you audition yet?"

"Soon."

"Break a leg!" shouted a bunch of people.

"Thanks." Claire smiled. "Who's there?"

"Everyone!" Layne sounded pleased. Claire could picture her narrow green eyes twinkling with delight. Her hair was probably scraggly and tangled. And her outfit was most likely a blinding combination of polyester prints and plaid man-pants. Not that it mattered. Layne Abeley was so much more than the sum of her outfits. She was a true friend, someone who loved to see her BFFs succeed, not fail.

"Who's everyone?"

"Me, Meena, and Heather."

Claire giggled. "Thanks, guys."

Massie and Alicia leaned against the Escalade, their eyes closed and their faces tilted toward the warm sun.

"Now remember one thing when you're auditioning." Layne sounded serious. "Don't *think* about the character, *become* the character."

"Got it." Claire closed her eyes, sealing the advice in her brain. "Thanks, Layne."

"Ew!" Alicia opened her eyes and pushed her wrap-around Ralph Lauren tortoiseshell sunglasses over her nose. "That's Layne?"

"We thought you were talking to Cam." Massie lowered her aviators from the top of her head. "Emma, we can leave."

"Very well." She began making her way across the parking lot toward the entrance.

"I better go," Claire said to Layne.

"Break a leg!" shouted the chorus.

"And call when you're done," Layne insisted.

"I will." Claire hung up the phone, then scurried to catch up to the others.

"Yoh audition is in an hour." Emma wrapped her hand around the door handle. "Use the time to familiarize your-selves with the script."

"Exactly what I was thinking." Massie twirled her charm bracelet.

Script? Claire was overcome by intense thirst. It felt like the inside of her mouth had been blasted with Massie's fifteen-hundred-watt hair dryer. In fifty-nine minutes they'd be standing in front of Rupert Mann auditioning for his movie. And she couldn't have felt less prepared.

"Um, can I ask a question?" Claire raised her hand tentatively.

Emma nodded.

"I was wondering if you could tell us about the character. You know, that we'll be reading for."

"Bloody 'ell." Emma's face flushed. "Did I not tell you?"

Claire shook her head.

"I'm glad one of us is thinking today."

"It's funny." Massie covered her heart with her hand. "I was about to ask the same thing."

"Me too." Alicia nodded.

"You'll be auditioning for Moh-lly Reynolds. An awwkward but cunning thirteen-year-old los-ah who hires someone to teach her how to be popular." Emma put her hand on her heart. "That's wheh yoh acting skills will come in. Because something tells me you three have no idear what it's like to be Moh-lly."

Massie and Alicia snickered.

Emma yanked the door open. "Welcome to Lakeview Middle School," she gushed. "Cool, roi-ght?"

The girls were standing in the middle of a hallway lined

with green lockers and glass cases filled with photos and trophies. Hand-painted signs reminding students about the upcoming dance hung from the ceiling, and Xeroxed flyers backing Marc Cooper for class president were scattered across the floor. It even had the same pencil-eraser-meets-tuna-sandwich smell that real schools have. Claire took out her camera and snapped a few shots for Cam while Emma got their VIP passes.

"Follow me." She handed them each a white-and-gold Gelding Studios sticker with their names on it, perfect to hang on their bedroom doors back home.

They followed Emma down the hall into one of the class-rooms. But when they stepped inside, they were no longer at Lakeview Middle School. They were back in Hollywood, surrounded by lights, cameras, and coils of thick black wire.

"This way." Emma led them into a small pantry. A fresh pot of coffee was brewing and a full box of doughnuts had been left beside it. "Help yoh-selves. I'll be right back with the scripts."

Claire went straight for the watercooler.

"Ehmagawd," Massie whisper-screeched. "Look!"

"Ehmagawd," Alicia echoed.

Claire almost spit up Poland Spring.

Right outside the pantry, with an unlit cigarette dangling from his fifteen-year-old lips, was *the* teen dream and renowned Hugo Boss underwear model, Conner Foley, typing a text message into his Sidekick. He had black spiked hair, olive-green eyes, and the tiniest hint of stubble on his face. He was just as good-looking in person as he was on the billboards in Times Square.

The hair-dryer thirst returned and Claire lifted the cup of water to her lips.

"Hey, Conner! Over here!" Massie shouted; then she and Alicia ducked behind the door. Conner turned and locked eyes with Claire. The water went down the wrong pipe and Claire started choking.

The actor yanked the unlit cigarette from his mouth, threw it on the studio floor, and crushed it with the heel of his black motorcycle boot.

"Conner's coming!" He rushed inside the pantry and began slapping Claire on the back. She wanted to tell him to stop but her mouth was full. The next slap did the trick. A stream of warm water shot out and soaked Claire's pink T-shirt.

Massie and Alicia cackled like witches.

Conner lifted his leather jacket and dabbed Claire's cheeks. The Mercedes key chain that hung from a belt loop on his customized CF jeans swayed.

Claire wanted to push him away from her and run back to the Escalade. Once he told Rupert what an unglamorous dork she was, Claire would have no shot at the role.

"Are those tears, babygirl?"

"No," she lied. "It's from the coughing."

He dabbed some more. "Poor thing."

Conner's face was so perfect, it hurt to look straight at it. Claire had to lower her eyes, as if staring into direct sunlight.

"Ehmagawd, are you okay, sweetie?" Massie put her arm around Claire.

"C'mere, you." Alicia held out her arms.

"I'm Massie, by the way." She held out her hand. "And you are?"

"I'm Conner Foley." He shook her finger. "The star of this film."

"Really?" Alicia batted her eyelashes. "We're auditioning."

"Oh, you're the nobodies Rupert is testing." He backed away from Claire. "I'll be running lines with you in an hour. I wanted my stand-in to do it, but you know Rupert: Everything has to be so friggin' real."

"That's so Rupe." Massie rolled her eyes.

"What's the scene about?" Alicia asked, batting her long lashes.

"I think it's the part where Molly tells Brad she's in love with him."

"Great," Claire groaned. How could she possibly face Conner again after spitting in his face?

"Oh, wun-dehful, I see you've met." Emma handed a script to each of the girls. "I mahk'd the pages you need to lehn. Rupert will be ready foh all of you in thurdy minutes. I'll be by to pick you up then."

"Thanks," the girls replied at slightly different times.

"Conner better cruise." He knocked the hollow wall, then turned on the heel of his motorcycle boot. "Later, babygirls."

"See ya," Massie chirped.

"Bu-yyyye," Alicia called after him.

"Ehmagawd!" They grabbed each other's wrists once he was gone.

"Did you really not know who I was?" Conner poked his head back in the room. "Or were you just playing?"

Massie and Alicia immediately let go of each other.

"We were just playing." Massie winked.

Conner bit his bottom lip and shook his head. "Oh, you *are* a devilish one." He shook his finger. "I better keep an eye on you."

"Yes." Massie batted her eyelashes. "You better."

"And on me too." Alicia stood up straight, revealing her ample cleavage. "I'm devilish too."

"Yes, you are." Conner popped another unlit cigarette in his mouth and turned down the hall.

Once they were certain he was gone, Massie and Alicia locked eyes, flapped their wrists, and silent-screamed for a good five minutes while Claire fanned her wet shirt with a Dunkin' Donuts box.

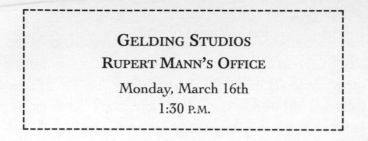

The inside of Rupert's office—which happened to be the house used in *Cellar Dweller* and *Cellar Dweller 2*—was more like a tribute to the director's career than a place of business.

"Look." Massie lifted a floppy straw hat off the "lucky bowling ball" that had been used in *Gutter Snipe* and put it on her head. "Who am I?" She tried to break into a model's strut but her path was obstructed by an eighteenth-century sofa, a cluster of beanbags, and two park benches. So she struck a pose instead. "Anyone?"

Claire and Alicia remained seated on the taxi seat used in *Roadblock*, their spines stiff and their eyes focused on the scripts in their hands.

"Come awn, you know this!" Massie took off the hat and put it on her head again.

Alicia looked up. "Uh, Jan Dandy from *Country Roads*."

"Yup." Massie put the hat back on the ball and scanned the room for another distraction.

There was a shelf full of rubber masks pinned to Styrofoam heads by the window, but she didn't feel like stepping over the piles of old *Variety* magazines to get to them. The last thing she needed was more sweat to roll down the backs of her knees. Why had she worn velvet pants on such a hot day? And why did Rupert insist on keeping his windows closed and his blinds open? She felt like she had been locked in a tanning booth. If Rupert didn't get back from lunch soon, the wax on her hair extensions would melt.

Massie brought her pinky to her lips, then lowered it before doing something she'd regret to her perfectly even nails. "Aren't you guys hot?"

The girls didn't even bother to lift their heads.

Massie eyed her script. It was on the heart-shaped night table (used during the dream sequence in *He Loves Me Not*), but she was too nervous to focus. Besides, she knew all of her lines. She even knew Conner's. And if *she* wasn't going to rehearse anymore, no one should.

"I know." She slapped her thigh, then began pacing. "Let's play What Would You Rather? Okay, what would you rather? A part in this movie or a two-year modeling contract?"

Alicia lifted her gaze. "A part in this movie."

"Kuh-laire?"

She was staring out the window, moving her lips like a mental patient.

"Kuh-laire! Enough memorizing," Massie snapped. "Which would you rather?"

"The movie." Claire returned to her pages.

Massie grabbed Rupert's "Best Director for *Waterlogged*" Oscar off his cluttered desk. "Okay, which would you rather?" She spoke into the statue's head as if it were a microphone. "A part in this movie, or to get back into OCD and get straight A's?"

She held the Oscar in front of Alicia's face.

"Would I have to try, or would the straight A's be automatic?" Alicia asked her script.

"Please, madame, speak into the mic." Massie pressed the Oscar against Alicia's lips. "Ew, you got gloss on his dome."

"Well, no one told you to mash it into my lips."

"Kuh-laire?" Massie put Oscar on Claire's script. "What would you rather?" She tilted him from side to side so it looked like he was asking the question. "Come on, tell me."

"So, I see you've met Oscar." Rupert stood in the doorway picking a piece of lettuce out of his teeth using the corner of an actor's headshot.

"I'm—I'm so sorry, I was just—"

"No woh-rries, glad you could make it." He reached into his distressed leather man-bag and pulled out Massie's purple-rhinestone-covered cell phone. "Hows 'bout you give me my baby and I'll give you yohs?"

Massie wiped the statue on her pants to clean Alicia's MAC Lipglass off Oscar's head. Once she handed it to Rupert, he dropped the phone into her palm.

When it landed, she felt a tingly sensation shoot up her arm. A few rhinestones were missing and the antenna was chipped, but it didn't matter. Holding the Motorola was like being with an old friend who'd stopped by to cheer her on. Massie squeezed it as hard as she could, hoping it would bring her luck.

"Shall we get stah-ted?" Rupert stuffed a stick of Big Red in his mouth.

The girls stood.

"Sit." He sank into a director's chair that said MR. MANN in stenciled white letters on the back. "I assume you know all yoh lines?"

Alicia and Claire nodded. Massie tightened her grip on the phone.

"Good, then." He flipped through the script. "While yoh acting, beh in mind that Moh-lly is desperately lonely and hasn't the foggiest on how to be cool. Her clothes ah pitiful, and her hai-h looks like it was cut with a spoon. Know what oy mean?"

Massie giggled, even though she didn't.

"The only thing this insec-uh gihl knows foh sho is that she's mad for a ninth gradah named Brad Douglas. In this scene, Molly tells Brad how she feels, hoping once he knows, he'll fall in love with her. Sound good, then?"

The girls nodded.

"Very well, then. Who wants to go first?"

"Me!" Massie's stomach fluttered and the backs of her knees flooded with sweat. But she refused to show how nervous she was. If Rupert didn't think she had confidence, he'd never buy her as a leading lady.

"Emma, we're ready fo-h Conn-ah!" Rupert called.

"Conner at your service." The spiky-haired actor shuffled in holding a brown paper bag in one hand and a torn page from the script in the other.

"Let's have you both ova th-eh by the south window, near the ficus. The light is puh-fect."

Massie took her mark.

"Rupert, line one," Emma called. "It's you-know-who."

Rupert took the call at his desk.

"Those are some hot pants you've got there, babygirl." Conner rubbed the back of his hand along the edge of Massie's thigh.

"Why, thank you." Massie fought the sudden urge to pee.

"No, I mean they're *hot* hot." Conner took a swig from his paper bag. "It's almost eighty degrees."

Alicia and Claire giggled nervously.

"Whatevs," was all Massie could think of to say.

Conner held out his bag. "You look like you could use a drink."

Massie caught a glimpse of the brown glass bottle inside. "No thanks." She waved him away. "I never do beer before an audition."

Conner pinched her pant leg. "Relax, Velvet. It's *root* beer."

"I know that, Rooty." He wasn't the only one who could come up with a nickname. Massie grabbed the bag out of his hand and pressed her lips on the exact spot where his lips had been.

"Thanks, Rooty."

"Welcome, Velvet."

Claire and Alicia shifted in their seats.

"Sorry 'bout that." Rupert sat. "Straightaway, please. And action!"

Conner suddenly turned his back to Massie and started twirling an invisible knob.

"What are you doing?" She rolled her eyes.

"*Cut!*" Rupert stuck two sticks of gum in his mouth. "The line is, 'Uh, Brad, can I talk to you for a minute?'"

"Oh." Massie blushed. "I didn't know we'd started."

"That's what 'action' means." Alicia laughed.

Thanks, Alicia. Do you know what "shut up" means?

"Straightaway aaaand, *action!*"

Conner fiddled again and Massie suddenly realized he was opening his imaginary locker. She marched up to him and tapped his shoulder.

"Brad, can I talk to you for a minute?"

"*Cut!* The line starts with, 'Uh, Brad.' Not 'Brraaaad.'" He said "Brad" in an exaggerated American accent.

"Sorry, I just thought the 'uh' made Molly sound too nervous."

"She's *supposed* to sound neh-vous." Rupert ran his hands through his thick hair. "Less thinking and more acting, please. *Action!*"

Conner began fiddling and Massie made her move.

"Uh, Brad, can I talk to you for a minute?" She put her hands on her hips.

"Depends who's askin'," Conner said to his "locker."

"My name is Molly." Massie rolled her eyes and folded her arms across her chest. "But I was hoping you already knew that."

"Why would I know that?" Conner looked her straight in the eye. "I've never seen you before in my life."

"Liar!" Massie smacked his arm. "Our mothers are best friends." She smacked him again.

"Cut!"

Massie smiled. She'd nailed it. That was why Rupert had stopped her early.

"Next!"

Alicia jumped up and quickly took her place.

"What'd you think?" Massie made sure to stand up straight as she walked back to her seat.

"I think you portrayed the loser as being incredibly self-assured and confident." Rupert spit a strawberry-size wad of gum in the trash and reached for the crystal bowl of cashews on his desk.

"Thanks." Massie beamed. She sank into the taxi seat and inhaled deeply to slow her speeding heart.

"Action!"

Conner fiddled.

Alicia crept up behind Conner. "Uh, Brad, can I talk to you for a minute?" she asked softly.

"Depends who's askin'," Conner said to his imaginary locker.

"My name is Molly." Alicia shifted nervously from one foot to the other. Then she twirled a piece of hair around her finger. "But I was hoping you already knew that."

"Why would I know that?" Conner looked Alicia straight in the eye. "I've never seen you before in my life."

"Liar!" Alicia knit her eyebrows, like she was confused and insulted at the same time. "Our mothers are best friends." She leaned toward Conner like she was pleading with him.

"I know: It's embarrassing, isn't it?" Conner tucked an imaginary binder under his arm and walked away.

"But wait!" Alicia called after him. "Wait." She lowered her head.

Rupert applauded. "Nicely done, love. Nice-ly done."

Massie decided Rupert was just saying that to make Alicia feel better because she'd acted like such a LBR.

"So?" Alicia smiled brightly.

"You really seemed to understand the character—"

Massie giggled.

"But you're too beautiful. I'm afraid no one would ever buy you as a loser." Rupert shook a handful of cashews into his palm like dice, then tossed them in his mouth.

"I'll drink to that!" Conner tilted his head back and took a drink from his bag.

"Thanks." Alicia smirked at Massie, then sat down.

"Whatevs," Massie smirked back. Did Rupert really think Alicia was beautiful, or was he trying to be nice?

"Next!"

The instant Claire stood up, Massie and Alicia burst out laughing. Her shirt had a big water stain right above her Hershey's Kiss–shaped boobs.

"Very interesting." Rupert unwrapped a stick of gum as he stared at Claire. "It ap-peas as though we have a method actress in ah midst."

Massie assumed "method" was Hollywood-speak for "mentally challenged."

"I admire the way you butch-ehd yo heh and stained yoh shu-ht for the au-dition." Rupert folded the gum like an accordion and pushed it into his mouth. "Very clev-ah."

"Yeah, you definitely look the part." Conner chuckled.

Massie and Alicia burst out laughing, then buried their faces in each other's shoulders.

Claire lowered her head and shut her eyes, like she was praying.

"*Action!*"

Conner fiddled.

Claire tugged on his shirt. "Uh, Brad, can I talk to you for a minute?" she mumbled.

"Depends who's askin'," Conner said to his locker.

"My name is Molly," Claire said to her thumbnail. "But I was hoping you already knew that."

"Why would I know that?" Conner looked Claire straight in the eye. "I've never seen you before in my life."

Claire shook her head frantically, like there was a bee buzzing in her ear. "Liar." She twirled a loose thread from her shorts around her finger until it turned purple. Then she ripped it off. "Our mothers are best friends." She was still looking down.

"I know: It's embarrassing, isn't it?" Conner tucked an imaginary binder under his arm and walked away.

"Wait!" Claire softly beckoned. "Wait." She gazed into the distance and wiped a lone tear off her pale cheek.

Massie's insides jumped for joy. There was no way Rupert would want a *real* loser in his movie. How would *that* look?

Claire sniffled. "Uh, do you have a tissue?"

"How about I have your assistant get that for you?" Rupert's face lit up. "Stella!"

Massie's ears started ringing. He was joking, right?

A thin Asian woman hurried in carrying a PalmPilot and a cell phone. Her long hair was tied in a neat bun and fastened with a pencil. She wore wide-leg trousers and a tight white tank top. Strings of turquoise beads hung around her neck and matched her strappy heels. If it weren't for the chocolate chip cookie she stuffed in her mouth, Massie would have assumed she was a model.

"Stella, could you please get this young lady a tiss-ue?" Rupert smiled like a proud parent.

"Here you go." She pulled a stack out of her pocket and handed it to Claire. "So, is she—?"

"Yes," Rupert interrupted. "This is Cl-eh Lyons. She will be replacing Hadley."

"*What?*" Massie heard herself shout. "You can't be

serious." Her face was burning like it was on fire, and she felt her entire body break out into a cold sweat.

Claire put her hand over her open mouth. "I don't believe it. Are you kidding?"

Rupert chuckled.

She looked around the room, her arms wide, like she was searching for someone to hug. But when no one came forward, she grabbed her own shoulders and swayed. "Thank you so much, Mr. Mann. You won't be disappointed."

"Call me Ru-pehrt."

Conner winked. "And call *me* later."

Massie swallowed hard as her entire social life flashed before her eyes. What would keep the girls at OCD loyal to her now? Or even the Pretty Committee? She pressed her hand against her mouth, not even caring that she was smudging her gloss.

Would Alicia, Kristen, and Dylan treat Claire like the alpha and *her* like the wannabe? Derrington would probably find another crush, someone more deserving of Briarwood's star goalie. And Claire Lyons would be rich, possibly richer than her!

She felt herself starting to hyperventilate and considered stealing Conner's brown bag so she could breathe into it. She always saw people doing that in the movies, but she figured with her luck she'd inhale the bag, choke on it, and die right there in front of everyone.

"Claire." Stella tapped her PalmPilot. "I have you double-booked for a few interviews this afternoon, so let me know which ones you want to do and which ones you want me to cancel. Also, Abby would like to meet you for dinner so she can get to know you better, and Ralph Lauren has invited you to raid the store. He'd like you to wear him exclusively while you are in town."

"What?" Alicia gasped. "Ralph is mine!"

"Ready to go?" Stella asked Claire. "The costume department is expecting you. They need your sizes."

Claire looked at Massie and Alicia with an ehmagawd-this-is-all-happening-so-fast expression. But the girls quickly turned away. "Can I call my mom?"

"From wardrobe." Stella put her arm around her and whisked her out of the office as though she were a pop star.

Massie watched Claire go, knowing for the first time in her life what it felt like to be the loser.

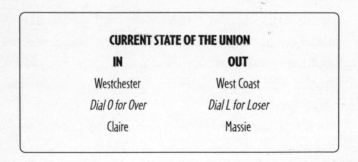

CURRENT STATE OF THE UNION

IN	OUT
Westchester	West Coast
Dial 0 for Over	*Dial L for Loser*
Claire	Massie

"Get me out of this garage sale." Massie zigzagged through the clutter in Rupert's office and marched straight out the door without saying goodbye.

"Where are you going?" Alicia called. "Wait up!" But Massie couldn't stop. Her legs had been programmed to move at high speeds when faced with a humiliating situation. And losing a part in a major motion picture to Claire Lyons certainly qualified.

The midafternoon sun was still blazing when she got outside, only it no longer felt warm and comforting on her skin: It burned.

"How are we going to get back to the hotel?" Alicia pushed through the swinging door, leaving it to stutter behind her.

They were at the back end of the studio lot surrounded by offices. The Lakeview Middle School set was miles away, which meant the front gates were even farther. Emma had driven them there in a golf cart, but she and her cart were long gone.

"Where's the Escalade?" Massie slipped on her aviators.

Alicia shrugged. "Where's our hotel?"

"This is in-sane!" Massie twisted her sweaty extensions

and piled them on top of her head. "I have never been without a driver. Never!"

The long road that led back to the soundstages was empty. No one was coming for them. "Gawd, this place is so unprofessional." Massie kicked the door and accidentally knocked the silver plate that said RUPERT MANN: DIRECTOR off its screw. It swayed back and forth, then fell onto the wood porch with a single clang.

Alicia burst out laughing.

"Hey!" someone shouted.

"Run!" Alicia screeched.

But there was nowhere to run except back inside the office, and Massie would rather have worn Laura Ashley than do that.

"Guys!"

This time the voice sounded familiar.

"Need a ride?" Claire and Stella hummed up to the curb in a Gelding golf cart. "I wasn't sure how you were getting back, so I asked Stella if we could check on you."

Luckily, Stella was too focused on her PalmPilot to see Massie blush.

"Yeah, we'd love a ride." Alicia turned to Massie. "Right?"

"Whatevs." Massie followed Alicia into the back of the cart, forced to stare at the back of Claire's conceited head.

"She better not take any pictures," she murmured to Alicia once they were moving. "Because I am so denying this."

"Point!"

"I can get you a ride back to Le Baccarat, but it won't be until four p.m.!" Stella shouted into the warm breeze while she drove. "I have to get Claire to wardrobe first. You don't mind waiting, do you?"

"It's fine." Massie folded her arms across her chest. "I have plenty of calls to return anyway."

Claire chewed her thumbnail.

"You are so lucky you're playing Molly." Stella smiled. "Or you would have to stop that biting."

"Phew." Claire wiped her forehead to show her relief.

Stella lifted one hand off the wheel and pinched Claire's cheek. "You are *too* cute."

Massie mocked their nauseating exchange by groping Alicia's face with exaggerated enthusiasm. They buried their laughter in their hands.

Minutes later, they were back in "Lakeview," only this time the massive set no longer seemed like an inevitable part of Massie's future. It had stopped being the place she would describe when interviewed about her first break. And it certainly didn't feel like her West Coast home away from home.

Lakeview Middle School was just a silly facade built by a bunch of glorified construction workers. It wasn't real. And neither was Claire's victory. Outside this fantasy world, she was nothing without the Pretty Committee. Massie told herself this over and over again as she followed Claire to the wardrobe room.

On the outside, the WR looked like another one of the

Lakeview Middle School classrooms, a wood door with a window covered by a drawn shade. But the inside was like nothing Massie had ever seen.

Ten long rows of clothing racks stretched from the entrance to the curtained dressing area in the back. And detailed index cards made it very clear which designers were among them. At a glance Massie saw DKNY, Ralph, Calvin, Dior, Theory, Juicy, L.A.M.B., C&C, Diesel, Citizen, Seven, True Religion, Ella Moss, and Joie. The footwear was displayed in neat rows along the back wall and seemed to include every possible sneaker, sandal, boot, flip-flop, and Ugg ever made.

"Welcome." A woman with a jet-black mullet and a deep tan smiled at them.

Massie pushed past her, hoping to get to the denim-covered couch in the middle of the room before she fainted. Alicia followed.

"I'm Ahnna." The woman's round gray eyes searched the girls, as if wondering where to land. "Now, which one of you is Claire?"

Stella put her hand on Claire's head. "This is."

"Nice to meet you." Claire smiled politely.

"Congratulations." Ahnna smiled back. She wore no makeup except for dark red lipstick, which had left its mark on the side of the Diet Coke can she was holding. "This is going to be so much fun." She pulled a tape measure from the side pocket on her camouflage cargo pants, which, to Massie's surprise, looked ah-dorable with her strappy gold heels, thin gold belt, and black tube top. A diamond heart was lodged in her belly button, inspiring Massie to add "navel jewelry" to her spring shopping list. "Claire, wait until you see all of the comps you and Abby are getting."

"Comps?" Claire's cheeks reddened.

"Free stuff—you know, from designers." Ahnna kicked a stack of boxes by the door with her heel. "It's been arriving all week. It *was* for Hadley, but now, my dear, it's all for you. I was going to have them sent to your hotel this afternoon. Is that okay?"

"Sure." Claire bobbed up and down on her tippy-toes.

"Hi, Ahnna." Massie stood. "I'm Massie, Claire's best friend."

"And I'm Alicia."

"How rude am I?" Stella covered her mouth. "I am so sorry. Yes, these are the other girls who tried out for Hadley's role."

"Ohhh, I'm sorry." Ahnna pouted.

"Do the runners-up get comps too?" Alicia asked.

"You know, like 'consolation comps'?" Massie made air quotes.

Ahnna looked at Stella, who looked at Claire.

"I'll share with you," Claire offered.

A cashmere-textured lump formed in Massie's throat.

"Great, let's get you measured." Ahnna turned on her iPod and the room filled with Natasha Bedingfield's optimistic pop. If ever there were a time to play Abby's angry rock, it would have been now.

Massie's stomach grumbled as she watched Claire spin from left to right, right to left, while Ahnna jotted measurements on the denim patches, which she was using instead of paper. "Puh-lease!" Massie sighed.

"Seriously." Alicia rolled her eyes.

"Her legs would be an inch smaller if she'd shaved this morning," Massie whispered.

Alicia burst out laughing.

Claire looked up, but Ahnna quickly turned her around and measured her neck.

"Do you have any special food requests?" Stella shouted above the music.

"Uh." Claire looked at Massie and Alicia, as if they were supposed to tell her what she liked to eat. "I like those Red Vines."

Stella tapped away on her PalmPilot.

"Are you allergic to any particular brand of makeup?"

"All of them," Massie snickered.

Alicia burst out laughing.

"Uh." Claire picked her cuticle. "Nope."

"And you're in the seventh grade, right?"

"Yup."

"Okay, your on-set tutor will be Mrs. Mendel. You'll start with her immediately. And I'll have a script delivered to you by messenger this evening. We start read-throughs tomorrow."

"Leesh," Massie said louder than she needed to. After all, Alicia was sitting right beside her.

"Yeah?"

"How excited are you to go back to New York?"

"I can't wait!" Alicia practically shouted. "I miss Josh."

"And I miss Derrington." Massie sighed.

Claire was staring at her bare feet, but Massie could tell by her vigorous nail-biting that she was listening to every word they were saying.

"I know," Massie continued. "When we get back, let's ask the boys if they want to go to a movie. How much fun would that be?"

"I heart that!"

"We could do it on Saturday," she suggested. "Friday night, during my sleepover, we'll pick our outfits and come up with a list of discussion topics—you know, so we won't have any weird silent moments."

"Heart!"

"We'll call them as soon as we get back to the hotel."

"Done."

Massie peeked at Claire out of the corner of her eye. She was scraping her chapped lips with her teeth and tugging on her short bangs. "Maybe you could do it again when I get back."

"Who knows when you'll be back?" Massie looked at her. "You'll probably end up moving here."

"No, I won't." Claire waved the ridiculous notion away. "This shoot is only three weeks long."

"You never know." Massie shrugged. "There are always

parts in movies for 'losers,' and after *Dial L*, everyone will think of you as a loser. Which means tons of work. You may never have time to go back to Westchester again."

"That's not true." Claire's shoulders drooped.

Ahnna pulled back her tape measure. "Posture."

"Sorry." Claire straightened up but kept her eyes fixed on the floor.

"Don't worry." Massie sweetened her tone. "Cam will never find a girl as good as you. He may try, but he won't succeed."

Claire knit her brows and turned away. Her tears were fastening their seat belts and preparing for takeoff.

Stella tossed her PalmPilot in her Fendi Spy bag as if it had personally offended her. Then she turned to face Massie. "Did you say Claire was your *best* friend?"

"Yup." She stole a quick glance at the boxes of comps by the door. "Why?"

"Well . . ." Stella leaned closer. "I think you might have upset her."

Alicia giggled.

"Puh-lease." Massie brushed off her comment with a dismissive wave, even though she knew Stella was right.

But what choice did she have? The girls at OCD were making new friends. Rupert had chosen Claire. And Derrington hadn't left her a single message since she'd gotten to Los Angeles. Life was going on without Massie Block. And the pain that came with that realization was much too agonizing to feel alone. It had to be shared.

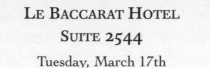

Red Vines for breakfast was probably *not* what Stella had meant when she said, "Change your diet." But chewing distracted Claire. And the last thing she wanted to think about was Massie and Alicia at the movies with Cam and the boys while she was left behind in L.A.

"I still don't see why you're leaving." Claire kicked the duvet cover off her legs and sat up.

"Because this town is D2M." Massie popped open one of her suitcases.

"It's dead to me too." Alicia zipped her brown Juicy hoodie.

It was early, too early for the sun. Claire grabbed the egg off the mirrored night table and pressed the button marked CURTAINS. The silk blinds parted, but the darkness made her feelings of isolation and loneliness stronger. She pressed the button again and watched as the drapes worked their way back together.

"You haven't even given it a chance." Claire bit down on Red Vine number twelve—or was it thirteen? "Remember how bored we were back home? You can swim here and look for celebrities. And it's not like you're missing school or anything."

"Puh-lease! I can't wait to get home." Massie crumpled her velvet pants in a ball and stuffed them in the bottom of her Louis. "I need to see Derrington before he forgets about me. You know what they say: 'Out of sight, out of mind.'"

The image of Cam sending gummy worms and C-notes to another girl made Claire gag. How long before he forgot about her? A month? A week? A day?

"I'll ask Rupert to hire you as extras," Claire tried. "Then you can be in the movie too."

"Extras?" Massie practically spit. "Kuh-laire, do I look like a deck of cards?"

She shook her head.

"Then what makes you think I want to get lost in the shuffle?"

Alicia drew an invisible number one with her finger. "Point!"

"I just think it would be fun if you stayed."

"Why don't you ask your assistant to find you some new friends?" Massie slammed her suitcase shut.

There was a knock on the door.

"I'll get it." Massie stepped over the piles of clothes and half-filled Louises on her way to open it.

"Morning," Judi practically sang.

"Are you girls almost ready?" Kendra fluffed her bob. "We should start making our way to the airport." She sat on the satin-covered couch, then sighed. "Our private-jet days are over. We have to check in with the airline two hours in advance."

"Do you really have to go?" Judi wiped her eyes, pretending to cry. "Who am I going to play with?"

"Oh, honeyyyyy." Kendra gave her a loving air hug.

Brrrring, brrrring.

Brrrring, brrrring . . .

Massie picked up the hotel phone. "Hello? . . . Hey, Kristen . . . Okay, hold on."

"What is it?" Claire jumped out of bed and hurried into the living room. Why was Kristen calling so early? Had Cam moved on?

"She wants us to turn on our iSight," Massie announced.

"I already packed the computer," Alicia whined from the bedroom.

"Unpack it," Massie insisted.

Alicia sighed. Minutes later her laptop was up and running on the entertainment console so they could sit on the couch while they spoke.

"Good morning." Kristen waved. She was leaning against Massie's bedroom desk, holding Bean. Dylan was beside her. They were both wearing black-tie sweats, and Kristen had an assortment of colored bobby pins on either side of her head.

Massie smiled for the first time all morning. "How's my puppy?"

Bean barked twice.

"It's time for your early-morning news report, coming live from Westchester at eight thirty in the morning." Dylan did her best anchor impersonation. "And here with the sports highlights is our very own Kristen Gregory."

"Thanks." Kristen handed Bean to Dylan. "Last night the Briarwood Tomahawks crushed the Forrester Ravens with a four–nothing win. After the game, temperatures dropped to an all-time low, forcing Derrington, the star goalie, to wear long pants for the first time ever."

"Ehmagawd, I can't believe I missed that!" Massie stomped her foot.

"How's Cam?" Claire pulled the sleeves on her Powerpuff Girls pj's over her hands. "Did you talk to him? Does he know I'm staying?"

Kristen and Dylan giggled.

"What?" Claire could feel her heart beating in her ears.

"We went out with the team for victory pizza." Dylan reached into a box of bran flakes.

"And talked about the St. Patrick's Day dance tomorrow night." Kristen twirled the string on her coral-colored sweatpants.

"And?" Claire had the sudden urge for one of Cam's gummy worms. But with only four left, she forced herself to hold off.

"And the guys said their new coach was making them go." Dylan paused. "With dates."

"What? Why?"

"He thinks that if they have crushes, their crushes will come to the games and they'll play harder—you know, to try and impress them," Kristen said.

"That's so stupid." Claire punched her thigh.

"How psyched are we that we're going back?" Massie asked Alicia.

"So psyched!" They high-fived.

Claire's fingertips felt cold. "How are you going to go? We're not allowed on school property."

"I'll find a way." Massie winked.

"Is Cam bringing anyone?" Claire asked.

"He *has* to." Dylan chomped.

Claire swallowed. "Who?"

"Dunno." Kristen shrugged. "He wasn't sure, you know, 'cause of you."

The combination of Red Vines and anxiety made Claire dry heave. Should she quit the movie and fly home? There were probably millions of girls who would love to take over for her, girls who weren't in love.

All of a sudden she felt her mother's warm hand on her back. Claire wiggled away to avoid bursting into tears.

"Hey, Kristen, are those my special-edition Uggs?" Massie asked.

"What? These?" Kristen smacked the top of the stud-covered purple boots.

"Yup," Massie smirked.

"I told you to aim the camera higher," Kristen whispered to Dylan.

"I thought I did!" Dylan whispered back.

"Uh, yeah. They kinda are." Kristen's pink cheeks turned red. "I figured since we had to go to your house to make this call, I might as well borrow a pair of boots. Besides, it's not like you need them. I mean, until you get home, right?"

"Well, we're coming home today so—"

"Wait, you are?" Dylan put Bean on the floor. "Why aren't you staying?"

Massie lifted her chin. "The director thought I was too confident to play a dork."

"And he thought I was too beautiful." Alicia batted her lashes.

Kristen and Dylan exchanged glances.

Claire was grateful the mothers were there or there would have been at least fifty comments about what a perfect loser Rupert thought she was.

"We thought you'd be all over the correspondent job." Dylan's green eyes were wide with disbelief.

"Huh?"

"Did you check your messages?"

"No," Massie snapped. "It's early here. The Razr is getting her beauty rest."

"Well, wake her up!" Dylan practically shouted.

Massie turned on her phone. She had fifteen messages. And they were all from Merri-Lee Marvil's show producers.

"My mom wants you and Alicia to be *The Daily Grind*'s behind-the-scenes reporters. You know, for *Dial L*."

Alicia gasped.

"Dylan, do I look like a video game?" Massie asked.

"No." Dylan smiled in anticipation.

"Then why are you playing me?"

"I'm serious. Your parents said it was okay." Dylan reached her hand in the cereal box.

"Surprise!" Judi and Kendra shouted.

"You knew about this?" Massie asked.

They nodded with pride.

"Didn't you wonder where my luggage was?" Kendra asked.

"No," Massie sneered. "I assumed it was with the luggage guy."

"Well, it's not!" Judi gushed. "You're staying. We all are!"

"Now that that's over . . ." Kendra stood. "We're going to grab some coffee downstairs." She blew her daughter a kiss on her way out. "Congratulations, sweetie."

"'Kay." Massie was obviously still absorbing the news.

Dylan inched closer to the camera. Her face filled the entire screen. "Every morning you'll go live from a different location on the *Dial L* set—you know, to give people a behind-the-scenes report."

"You can even interview the stars," Kristen added.

"Ehmagawd!" Alicia hugged Massie. "This is even better than my old reporting job at OCD!"

Massie remained calm. "Why is your mom doing this?"

"Because it's the first time a major Hollywood movie has cast a lead with no experience. So she wants to do a whole Amateur's Week–type thing."

"What do you mean, 'no experience'?" A sinister grin appeared on Massie's face.

Claire rolled her eyes.

"They're even giving you an expense account and your own camera crew." Kristen sounded distant, even a little sad. "You're going to have so much fun."

"Dial Y for Yay!" Alicia shouted, obviously not caring that it sounded totally stupid.

"Wait, how did you know we didn't get the part in the movie?" Massie paced. "I didn't tell anyone."

"Me either." Alicia glared at Claire.

"Claire left a message for Cam and he—"

"Aha!" Massie cut Kristen off. "You just couldn't wait to rub it in, could you?" Her amber eyes practically seared a hole through Claire's skull.

"I wanted to tell him I wouldn't be coming home for a while. I wasn't trying to—"

"We would have known anyway," Kristen said. "It's all over the news. The press thinks it's a big deal that Rupert cast a nobody."

"Can everyone please stop saying that word?" Claire heard herself shout.

"Would you prefer *loser*?" Massie asked.

Claire covered her face with a satin pillow.

"Let's do it! Let's stay. Come awn, Mass!"

Massie tapped her chin. "Hmmmmm."

"Come awn!" Alicia whined.

The room was silent.

"Please?"

"O-kkkayyyyy," Massie said.

Bean barked.

"Pack your bags, puppy," Massie cooed. "You're coming to Hollywood."

Bean barked again.

"No fair," Kristen whimpered.

"I know," Dylan moaned.

"Yayyyyyy!" Alicia shouted.

Massie yanked the pillow off Claire's face.

"Happy now? You got your wish. We're staying."

Claire chomped down on her last Red Vine, vowing she'd never *ever* wish for anything again.

A beauty buffet of hair and makeup products by MAC, Nars, Chanel, Benefit, Hard Candy, Tarte, Dior, Dessert, and Paul Mitchell surrounded Massie and Alicia. They were seated in directors' chairs facing a mirror that was lit by round bulbs, getting their faces put on for their first appearance on *The Daily Grind*.

"Is there any way this trailer could be moved to our hotel?" Massie asked Gina, their makeup artist.

"Seriously." Alicia blew on her vanilla steamer. "We had to wake up at five a.m. to get here on time. And no one looks good at five a.m. Not even us." She giggled.

"That's what I'm here for." Gina unscrewed a tube of Nars lip gloss. "Close," she told Massie.

"Whoever came up with this whole time-difference thing is D2M," Massie murmured. "When Merri-Lee asked us to be on her show at nine-thirty a.m., did she realize it would be six-thirty a.m. *here*?"

"Stop talking!" Gina snapped. "How do you expect me to gloss you when your lips are moving?"

"Mmm-mmm," Massie apologized to the petite blonde. But seriously, how could she be expected to look and feel her best at this ungawdly hour? Of all the times she'd imagined addressing the nation on live TV—and there had been many—never once had Massie pictured herself with dark circles under her eyes (or sharing the spotlight with Alicia!). But for a first-time gig, Hollywood correspondent for *The Daily Grind* wasn't bad. At least that was what Massie told herself when she looked out the window and saw Claire and Abby laughing their way out of a stretch limo.

Massie leaned into her reflection. "Do you think I look like Jennifer Ho-pez with all this makeup caked on my face?"

"I didn't *cake* it on." Gina dusted Massie's lids. "Besides, this is TV, not prom. If your makeup isn't dark, the lights on the camera will wash you out and you'll look anemic."

"Given," Alicia agreed with Gina. "I did the news at my old school. I know all about that whole dark-makeup thing."

"You were on the PA system," Massie snapped.

"I still had to wear makeup."

"Where? On your tonsils?"

Gina cranked the volume on her iPod. Groovy lounge music flowed out of her portable speakers and Alicia made a peace sign and swayed like a hippie. Massie burst out laughing. So what if her makeup was cakey? This was better than sitting in Westchester waiting for some stupid board meeting.

"Are you nervous?" Alicia asked.

"Me? Not at all. You?"

"Nope." Alicia shook her head one too many times. "I was born to anchor. I can't wait." She pushed up the sleeves on her navy blue RL blazer. "Why, are you?"

"Nope." Massie wiped her clammy hands on the canvas seat below her butt.

"Do you think Ralph Lauren will give *us* clothes, you know, now that we're going to be famous too?" Alicia cemented her blowout with a blast of Paul Mitchell Freeze and Shine Super Spray.

"Ew, do you really want to wear Ralph if Claire is?"

"Hold still!" Gina gripped Massie's jaw and repositioned her face.

"Point." Alicia sighed.

Someone pounded the outside of the trailer door. "Special delivery for Miss Maysee Block."

A stocky man in brown shorts and a brown starchy shirt stepped into the trailer. He was carrying a crate with American Airlines stickers all over it.

"Bean!" Massie grabbed the crate and opened the gate. The black puppy ran around in small circles and then jumped into her open arms.

"Sign." The delivery guy shoved a clipboard in front of Massie's face and handed her a chewed Bic pen.

"Can we please finish up here?" Gina held a mascara wand above Massie's lashes. "You know you're going live in, like, ten minutes, right?"

Massie nodded.

"And you know I have to finish your eyes, right?"

All of a sudden, the realization of what she was about to do hit her. Hard. In less than ten minutes Massie would be addressing millions of viewers, whether she was ready to or not. The only direction Merri-Lee had given her was "Act natural." There were no lines to learn or marks to hit. All they had to do was chat with the stars and show the viewers at home some of the cool behind-the-scenes action.

"It'll be easy," Merri-Lee promised. "Just like talking to your friends."

Massie reached into the pocket of the new Frankie B. jeans and clutched her lucky cell phone. Bean was on her lap, her best friend was at her side, and a professional was applying her makeup.

She was ready for her close-up. Not that she had a choice.

"Now remember," instructed Hal, the *Daily Grind* producer assigned to Massie and Alicia. "When I count you in I'll say, 'In three, two,' and then I'll point. I won't say 'one.'"

Massie did her best to concentrate, but Hal's overly hairy arms were making it difficult. The least he could have done was worn long sleeves.

"So you're saying we won't *hair* you say 'one.'" Massie fought her quivering lips.

Alicia burst out laughing.

"Exactly." Hal smiled. "And when it's time for you to wrap up, I'll twirl my finger in the air like this." His index finger made several rotations.

"You'll twirl your finger in the *hair*," Alicia smirked. "Got it."

"Now remember, this is live. There are no do-overs."

"'Kay." Massie wondered if she should have worn a dress instead of her beige Lauren Moffat Bermuda shorts and a colorful knit Mossimo cami. Her outfit was great, but was it TV-great or just school-great? She would have to speak to Merri-Lee about hiring a wardrobe person. Poor Alicia had changed nine times before settling on a pair of skinny Paige jeans and a yellow-and-orange Charlotte Ronson ruffle top.

"Okay, girls." Hal rubbed the thick patches of black stubble on his cheeks. "Two minutes. Let's get you in position."

Massie's stomach lurched.

"Let's have you standing in front of the classroom." Hal opened the door, revealing the chaos and clutter backstage. He turned to the cameraman. "Jimmy, give me plenty of behind-the-scenes action, but don't forget to cover the school set. I want both."

"Copy that." Jimmy hoisted the camera onto his shoulder.

Massie's stomach lurched again. This was really happening.

"Girls, do you want to go over the script one last time?" Hal asked.

Massie took in a deep breath. "Sure." She exhaled slowly. "First we thank Merri-Lee; then we introduce ourselves and tell everyone where we are."

"Then we talk about the movie and how we'll be live from the set all week interviewing the stars and spreading tons of behind-the-scenes gossip," Alicia added.

"After that, we say goodbye to Merri-Lee, who is back in New York, and tell her we'll see her tomorrow." Massie rolled her shoulders. "Done, done, and done."

"Perfect." Hal gave Jimmy the thumbs-up. "We're all set. You're a couple of naturals."

"I used to do this all the time for my school." Alicia fluffed the ruffles on her shirt.

"And I'm just a natural." Massie spit her gum onto her script and tossed them both in the trash.

"Okay, then," Hal said to his stopwatch. "Have great show, everyone."

Alicia grabbed Massie's wrist with her clammy hand.

"Ew!" Massie wiped her arm on Alicia's jeans.

"Get away!" Alicia jumped back.

Massie giggled, but it sounded like it was coming from someone else. The back of her neck started to sweat, and she felt strangely detached from her body—like she was watching herself on iSight.

"Ready?" Hal handed them each a *Daily Grind* microphone. They were heavier than they looked, and Massie's mic kept sliding through her sweaty palms. She tightened her grip and shifted her weight to her right foot. Then her left. Then her—

"Here we go!" Hal shouted like they were preparing to jump out of an airplane. "We're live in three . . . two . . ." He shook his pointer finger as if it were covered in sticky boogers.

The red light on top of Jimmy's camera popped on.

Alicia burst out laughing.

Massie begged her mouth to speak. But it refused. Merri-Lee had lied. The black lens of the camera looked nothing *like* her friends. It was more like an angry, soul-sucking cyclops that glared at her expectantly and said, "I'm bored.

Entertain me. Come on. Do it. I dare you. Do it. Entertain me. Do it. Do it. *Now!*"

"Say something," urged Hal. "We're live."

Alicia laughed harder.

"Talk about the movie," he pleaded. "Please!"

Alicia doubled over in hysterics, and two tears streamed down her face.

"The movie!"

Massie could hear him; she just couldn't respond. It was like her entire body had been Botoxed.

Hal waved at someone backstage, silently begging the person to come over.

Massie wanted to turn her head to see who it was, but the scared-stiff thing was still happening.

"Hey, guys." Claire squeezed between Massie and Alicia.

"Say something." Hal immediately tossed her a microphone. Claire caught it and smiled confidently. She smelled like fruity hair spray and peppermint ChapStick.

"Hey, I'm Claire Lyons and I'm standing on the set of *Dial L for Loser*. My friends Massie and Alicia were just demonstrating what a real loser would act like: Hope you didn't think they were serious." She winked at the camera.

Hal gave her an enthusiastic thumbs-up.

And just like that, Massie reentered her body. She wasn't about to stand there and watch Claire hijack her chance at fame a second time.

"Ehmagawd!" Massie rubbed her lips together to make sure they were still glossed before continuing. "Give the audience some credit, Kuh-laire. They're not stupid. They knew we were joking." She elbowed Alicia in the ribs. "Right?"

"Given." Alicia wiped her mascara-stained cheeks.

From that moment on, Massie imagined she was speaking to Dylan and Kristen. And just as Merri-Lee had suggested, the words came. "We're standing in the 'halls' of 'Lakeview Middle School,' where—"

Alicia cut her off. "Well, they're not really *halls*. This whole thing is a set. It's fake."

"*Claire Lyons to wardrobe. Claire Lyons to wardrobe,*" a voice boomed over the loudspeaker.

"That's me." Claire beamed. "Hey." She looked straight into the camera. "Wanna check out the wardrobe room?"

Jim moved the camera up and down like it was nodding. Claire giggled. "Follow me."

Massie stepped in front of her. "Right this way." She guided the audience through a maze of lights and wires. "We are now 'behind the scenes.'" Her use of air quotes made the producer smile. She was back! "And if you're lucky, we'll see Conner Foley or Abby Boyd walking around. I hung out with them the other day and they promised me an interview later in the week, so make sure you stay tuned for that."

Finally, Massie got a thumbs-up of her own. How could she have been so nervous? This hosting thing was easy. Dial V for VJ!

"Well, I'm here with one of the stars right now." Alicia

grabbed Claire's arm. "She will be playing Molly, the loser. You should see her. She's a real natural. Isn't that right?"

"Uh, I wouldn't say *that*." Claire smiled. "Our first day of shooting is today, so we'll see."

Massie quickened her pace, hoping Alicia and Claire would fall out of the frame. But Claire kept talking and the camera stayed on her.

"Here we are outside the wardrobe room." She pointed to the denim *W* and the denim *R* that Ahnna had tacked to the center of the door. "It's time for me to change into my Lakeview Middle School uniform." Claire reached for the handle and noticed a shiny silver box at her feet. "What's this?" It had a red ribbon tied around it and a card with her name on it. She looked around, obviously wondering if this was some sort of prank. "Should I open it now?" Claire asked the camera.

"Let's not forget, this is *The Daily Grind*, not *The Claire Lyons Show*." Massie did her best to sound playful.

The producer checked his stopwatch. "Open it," he whispered.

Claire shrugged, then tore the wrapping. "Oops, I should probably read the card first." She giggled.

Random crew members gathered, smiling expectantly.

"'To Claire,'" she read. "'Welcome to Hollywood! Love, the cast and crew of *Dial L for Loser*.'" Her hand was on her heart, as though she was so touched, she could cry at any moment.

Puh-lease!

"Ehmagawd!" Claire shouted once the last bits of wrapping paper were on the ground.

Massie gasped. "Ehmagawd" was *her* expression.

"How ah-dorable!" Claire held up the gift. It was a special-edition *Dial L for Loser* Motorola. The whole thing was covered in red rhinestones, except for the back, which said CLAIRE in tiny pearls. Inside, the number-five key, the one with the letter *L* on it, was made of gold. "This is ah-mazing! Thank you!"

"She *can* act," Massie whispered to Alicia. "Like *us*!"

"Seriously!"

The crew applauded and the camera whipped around to capture the sentimental moment.

"Dial P for Phony," Massie whispered to Alicia.

Hal started circling his finger, and Massie remembered that gesture from the first grade; it meant "whoop-dee-doo!" He ahb-viously thought Claire was showing off too.

"Okay, so, getting back to the tour," Massie addressed the camera, which finally panned back onto her. "I'm going to take you inside the wardrobe room for an exclusive look at the costumes. There are at least a thousand pairs of shoes in there."

The producer kept doing that thing with his finger.

Massie ignored him while opening the door to the wardrobe room and practically knocking Ahnna to the ground.

"Oh, hi, Ahnna." Alicia nudged Massie out of the way.

"You can't come in here." Stella held her clipboard in front of her face. "This is a cast-only room."

Massie turned to the producer and gave him a "fix this!" glare.

The producer was "whoop-dee-do"-ing even faster.

"What?" Massie snapped.

"Wrap. It. Up!" he whisper-yelled.

"Oh, right." Massie blushed. "Tune in tomorrow, because we'll have a lot more behind-the-scenes action from the new movie—"

"*Dial L for Loser.* I'm Alicia Rivera and that was Massie Block and we heart you! See you tomorrow. Back to you, Merri-Lee."

The red light above the camera went dim.

"Wonderful!" the producer shouted. He raced over to Claire and hugged her. "You saved us. Thank you."

"No problem," Claire murmured into his hairy chest. When he finally let go, she ran over to Massie and Alicia.

"You guys were great." She smiled genuinely.

Massie opened her mouth but nothing came out. She didn't know who to yell at first: Claire for stealing the show, Alicia for stepping all over her lines, or the producer for distracting them with his silly hand gestures. The only thing she knew for sure was that she'd call an emergency meeting with her crew to make sure none of the above ever happened again. That was, if Merri-Lee didn't fire them first.

"Okay, you." Stella rested her hand on Claire's shoulder.

"We have to get you dressed, run you over to makeup, and rehearse your scene. Oh, and the reporter from *Access Hollywood* wants five minutes with you before we start shooting at two p.m."

Claire rolled her eyes at Massie and Alicia, pretending to be unenthused about her day. But Massie knew she was just doing that so they wouldn't think she was starting to get a big head.

Too late!

"Oh, and which one of you is Massie?" Stella was still scanning her clipboard.

"I am." Massie raised her hand. She knew if she hung around the set they'd offer her a role.

"Please report to the makeup trailer." Stella crossed something off her list. "Gina wants you to pick up your dog ay-sap. He just peed all over her brushes."

Alicia and Claire giggled.

"*She*." Massie stomped her foot. "And her name is Bean."

"That's not what Gina called her." Stella yanked Claire into the wardrobe room, then slammed the door in Massie's face.

┌───┐
│   GELDING STUDIOS   │
│   THE *DIAL L FOR LOSER* SOUNDSTAGE   │
│   BACKSTAGE   │
│   Wednesday, March 18th   │
│   7:20 P.M.   │
└───┘

"Hey, Cam, it's me." Claire mouthed goodbye to three extras in Lakeview Middle School uniforms as they passed her.

"See ya tomorrow, Claire," one of them gushed. "It was *so* nice meeting you."

"You were really good today," added another.

Claire smiled and pointed to her new special-edition *Dial L for Loser* phone, letting them know she would have thanked them if she hadn't been mid-message.

"Uh, anyway, where was I?" Claire rubbed her head. Her hair was sticky and coarse from too much hair spray. "Oh yeah, happy St. Patrick's Day. I guess you're going to the dance so, uh, have fun. I wish I was there. Believe me. School was so much easier. I've had the longest day ever." She giggled. "Anyway, I miss y—, uh, Westchester. Call me later. Oh, have fun tonight. Wait. Did I already say that?" She giggled again. "Sorry, I'm so tired. 'Kay, I'm going now. Bye."

Claire wanted to tell him she loved him and missed him and couldn't wait to lip-kiss him when she got home. But for all she knew, he was slow-dancing with another girl right now. So all she said was, "Call me, you know, when you get this message. Or when you have a minute. Or whenever. 'Kay? 'Kay. Bye. Again." She hung up and sat on an empty camera case.

Her entire body throbbed. It had been a long day of script-reads, scene-blocking, and endless introductions to people whose names she'd already forgotten. And now that she finally had a moment to relax, all Claire could think about was Cam and the rich, beautiful, popular girl who was probably pressing the tip of her nose against his Drakkar Noir–scented neck at this very moment.

She flipped open her phone and dialed a new number, loving the way the red rhinestones felt against her palm.

"Hello?"

"Layne?"

"Lyons?"

"Yeah!" Claire forgot about her aching feet.

"How's it going? Have you met Conner? How is Abby? Is she being nice to you? I miss you! I wish you were going to be at the dance tonight. But wait, no, I don't. I'm glad you're there. You know, for you. But I wish you were going to the dance."

"I know. Me too." Claire's feet went back to aching. "Who are you going with?"

"Meena and Heather." Layne giggled. "We're going to dominate!"

"Who's Cam taking?"

"Dunno." Layne suddenly sounded rushed. "Wait! My brother Chris is backing out of the driveway as we speak. Oh my Gawd, *Chris! If you leave without me, I'll*—Claire, I gotta go. I'll call you from the dance with a full Cam report. *Chris, get back*—"

The line went dead. Claire sat and listened to the silence on the other end for a full minute before hanging up.

Cl-eh, Cl-eh.

Cl-eh, Cl-eh.

She snapped out of her daze and flipped open her phone, which bleated Rupert's voice every time it rang. It was something he insisted on, and Claire certainly wasn't going to object. It wasn't every day an Oscar-winning director volunteered to record her ringtone.

Cl-eh, Cl-eh.

Cl-eh, Cl-eh.

"Hey!" She tried to sound upbeat in case it was Cam.

"Where are you?" shouted the girl on the other end. Ciara's "1, 2 Step" was blasting in the background.

"Layne?" Claire jumped to her feet. "Are you at the dance already?"

"Who?" The music on the other end got louder. So loud, in fact, that it sounded like it was coming from the other end of the hall.

"It's me, freak-a-dee!"

"Me"? Claire wondered, wishing she had taken the time to program everyone's numbers into her new phone. Maybe then she'd know who she was speaking to.

"Where you at, kitty cat?"

"Abby?" Claire felt funny saying the actress's name. After all, they had only known each other for one full day. And most of it had been spent reading nasty lines to each other during rehearsals.

"Yes, it's Abby!" she shouted. "Wherefore art thou?"

"Backstage. You?"

"Wardrobe room."

Ahnna woo-hooed and Abby cracked up. "Get your butt in here. We have an eight p.m. rez at Boi, which means we have ten minutes to get fabulicious before the limo gets here."

"Are you serious?" Claire had no idea where Abby got her energy. "Aren't you tired?"

"Tired of not being on the scene, jelly bean." Abby added a "woo-hoo" for effect. "Let's go!"

"I'm on my way." Claire hung up and weaved her way past the dozens of crew members who were coiling cables and draping blankets over cameras so they could finally head for home.

Claire thought about the big, soft bed in her suite and the mini cheeseburgers from room service and instantly regretted answering her phone. But Massie and Alicia were probably there trying on outfits for tomorrow's *Daily Grind* segment, and Cam . . . Well, she had no idea what he was doing. So maybe a night on the town with Abby Boyd was just what she needed.

Without further hesitation, Claire dialed her mother.

"Are you all done for the day?" Judi asked.

"Yup."

"How was it?"

"Good. Long but good." Claire grabbed a handful of Red Vines off the craft service table.

"I want the details over dinner." Judi sounded giddy. "I'm with Kendra and the girls right now. We're thinking of going to—" She pulled away from the phone. "What's the name of that spot?"

"Asia de Cuba," Kendra said. "In the Mondrian Hotel."

"Asia de Cuba," Judi repeated. "It's in some fancy-shmancy hotel."

"Uhm." Claire took a deep breath. "Well, Abby kind of asked me to go to dinner with her." Claire exhaled. "I think it's kind of a get-to-know-you thing. But if you don't want me to go I—"

"Don't be silly. Go! Have fun with Abby!" Judi pulled away from the phone again and started speaking to some-one else. "What, dear? Oh . . . Well, why don't you ask her yourself? Here she is."

Claire's stomach clenched.

"Kuh-laire?" Massie said. "Hey, how was your day?"

"Not bad. Yours?" Claire couldn't help holding back. The girls had been ignoring her ever since she'd helped them with their *Daily Grind* segment, and she knew better than to think they were suddenly over it.

"Great! We worked out a lot of the kinks and tomorrow's show is going to be ah-mazing."

"Good." Claire stopped outside the wardrobe room. Nelly's "Grillz" was blaring at top volume.

"So *what* are you doing tonight?" Massie asked, like Claire had already told her but she'd forgotten.

"Oh, I'm having some dinner thing with Abby." Claire did her best to sound casual so she couldn't be accused of bragging.

Massie whispered something, probably to Alicia.

"Listen." Massie pressed her mouth against the phone. "We totally need a break from the mothers."

Claire's chest tightened. She knew what was coming next.

"Do you think we could meet up with you guys?"

"Uh, I'm not sure where we're going," Claire lied. "Let me check with Abby and I'll call you back."

"Awesome!" Massie whispered something else to Alicia. "Call me back, on my phone."

"'Kay. Oh, and tell my mom I'll be home by ten thirty and that the limo will drop me off."

"'Kay. Call me back." Massie hung up.

Claire bit into a Red Vine and closed her eyes while she chewed. Why had her mother put Massie on the phone? Now Claire *had* to include her. And that meant a night of loser jokes at her expense.

"Hey." Claire pushed open the door to the wardrobe room. She wanted ten humiliation-free minutes with Abby Boyd. Then she'd call.

"Heyyyyy," Claire called again, but Abby and Ahnna were in the back by the mirrors and couldn't hear her. "HEYYYYYY!"

"Claire!" Abby jumped up on the denim couch. "Whaddu'ya think? Do you like?" She twirled so quickly, her sparkle-covered skirt puffed out like an umbrella.

"You look ah-mazing!" Claire remembered the faded blue

T-shirt dress she'd worn to the set and thought about going out in her Lakeview uniform. It was much sexier.

"Ahnna made the skirt herself." Abby jumped down.

"Well, I just added the sparkles." Ahnna shrugged. "It was easy. Abby was the genius who paired it with the bikini top and jean vest."

"If I knew we were going out tonight I would have put something together from the comp boxes, but—"

"Relax." Ahnna applied a fresh coat of red lipstick. "Abby and I already pulled something for you. If you don't like it, there's tons more to choose from."

"Seriously?"

"Absolution," Abby replied with a proud smile.

Ahnna ran off for a second and reappeared with three hangers. The first held a tiny pair of gold shorts; the second, a faded vintage rock tee that said JOURNEY on the front; and the third, a wide leather belt.

"You're not serious, are you?" Claire had underwear bigger than those shorts.

"Try it!" Ahnna stomped her foot in fake frustration.

Claire bit her thumbnail.

"Go!" Ahnna thrust the clothes into Claire's arms.

"Why not, right?" She giggled and headed for the curtain.

She slid the shorts on under her pleated skirt and was surprised by how easily they fastened. The shirt was much tighter, but deliciously soft. And the belt slithered through the generous loops on the shorts and buckled with ease.

"Come out, we wanna see!"

Claire wiggled out of her uniform and yanked the curtain aside, anxious to see herself in the mirror.

Abby's and Ahnna's mouths hung open.

"What?" Claire's cheeks burned. "Are the shorts up my butt? Do I look fat? Should I have shaved my thighs? I did my calves but stopped at my thighs because—"

"You look foxy," Ahnna mused.

"Like a roller-derby rocker!" Abby punched the air.

"Slip these on." Ahnna handed Claire a pair of Frye cowboy boots made from the same brown leather as the belt.

"And these." Abby hung a long string of wooden beads around Claire's neck. "Wow."

"Claire, your legs look so long." Ahnna sighed with a touch of envy.

"Positively giraffic!" Abby twisted a yellow-stone ring off her pinky and handed it to Claire. "Here, take this."

"I can't." Claire shook her head.

Abby wiggled her ring-covered fingers. "I think I can spare one."

"Seriously?" Claire took the ring and carefully slid it onto her pinky, as if it held the secrets of the universe.

"Twist the stone."

Claire did what she was told and the ring popped open. Inside was a tiny pot of gold-speckled gloss.

"It matches your shorts." Abby grinned.

"I love it." Claire breathed in the caramel smell as she smeared it across her lips.

"You look like Hollywood royalty." Abby smiled.

"I feel like it." Claire hugged Abby, then Ahnna. "Thank you both."

Finally, Claire understood why the Pretty Committee was so obsessed with their outfits. She felt *special* dressed as a "roller-derby rocker"; unstoppable, beautiful, and alluring. But that was on the outside. Underneath the fabulous clothing she was still an insecure girl, dying to know why her crush wasn't returning her call.

Claire peeked at her phone. The display said 0 MESSAGES.

"One more thing." Ahnna came at her with a palmful of coconut-scented gel. She rubbed it between her fingers, then separated Claire's bangs into spiky pieces. "Now you're done."

"I want some of that." Abby pouted.

"C'mere." Ahnna ran her gelly fingers through Abby's short blond hair until it was full of twists, points, and intentional tangles.

"Conner's turn," announced the actor, closing the door behind him.

"What are you doing here?" Abby's hazel eyes brightened. "I told you we'd meet you in the limo."

"He's coming?" Claire whispered to Abby.

She nodded. "Is that okay?

"Of course!" Claire said a little too quickly. "I mean, sure. Why not?"

"Conner needs a blazer." He put his arms around Ahnna's narrow hips and kissed her on both cheeks. "I can't go out with two hot babygirls looking like this."

"Let's go." Ahnna pulled him toward the men's section.

Claire checked her phone again—still no messages. She was tempted to take a picture of herself and send it to Cam but decided to wait until he called back. Whenever that might be.

Instead, she took a deep breath and dialed Massie. It had been more than ten minutes since they spoke and she was probably fuming. Claire was about to hit send but stopped. *I'll call after the next song,* she told herself. Then she pressed store.

"Last one in the limo rides without underwear!" Conner yelled. He pushed open the door and took off down the hall.

Claire and Abby screamed, then raced out after him.

"Thanks, Ahnna!" Claire called over her shoulder.

"Pleasure." Ahnna chuckled. "Have fun!"

If Claire had been wearing her Keds she would have passed Conner, but the boots must have weighed five pounds and made her feel like she was jogging underwater. Still, she refused to spend her first night out in L.A. without underwear. It was too cliché.

"Start stripping!" she yelled when she passed Abby.

"Nooooo fairrrr." Abby cracked up. "I'm in heels."

Claire ran outside, dashed through the lot, and smacked the back of the limo.

"Nice running, babygirl." Conner tossed an unlit cigarette in his mouth. "Guess those legs of yours work as good as they look."

Claire turned away before he saw her blush. "Where's Abby?"

She felt a tap on her shoulder and whipped her head around, smashing right into the actress. "Ahhhhhh!"

"Ahhhhhhh!" Abby screamed back.

They burst out laughing.

A uniformed driver opened the door and everyone slid inside. Flashing blue lights wrapped around the ceiling and pulsed to the beat of the club music that Conner cranked on the radio.

"Take. It. Off!" he chanted as the driver pulled out of the lot. "Take. It. Off!"

Claire could hardly look at Abby, she was so embarrassed. How was she going to get out of this?

But without hesitation, Abby reached under her skirt, slid off her black thong, and whipped it at the security guard as they drove through the gates.

Claire and Conner burst into hysterics at the sight of her underwear flying toward the guard's face and landing on his cap.

"I can't believe you did that," Claire managed to say when she finally caught her breath. Her stomach ached from laughing so hard.

"Babygirl, you are wild!" Conner pushed back the sleeves of his black corduroy blazer.

Claire checked her phone while they relived the moment the guard swatted the dangling thong off his head.

It was almost eight o'clock and still there were no messages from Cam.

OMG! Massie!

Claire was supposed to call her twenty-five minutes ago. She quickly pulled up her number and her thumb hovered over the send button, but for some reason she couldn't press it.

"Who are you calling?" Conner leapt across the seat and squeezed beside her. He smelled like shaving cream.

"Just a friend." She sighed.

"Not a boyfriend, right?" Conner pressed his knee against Claire's bare leg and burrowed deep into her soul with his olive-green eyes. Her intestines did a three-sixty. *Was Conner Foley flirting with her?*

"Nope, just a friend." Claire closed her phone. "She was going to meet us out, but I think it's too late now."

"Then you won't mind if Conner takes that." He placed his warm hand on hers. Thin bolts of electricity shot up her arm as he slid the phone out from under her clammy palm and dropped it in the back pocket of his CF jeans. "You have been checking that thing all night. And Conner is jealous."

Claire giggled. He couldn't possibly mean that, could he?

"We're here!" Abby popped open her green ring and pulled out a mint. "Want one?" she offered.

"No thanks." Claire gripped her stomach when she saw the cluster of paparazzi surrounding the limo. "Are they here for you?"

"For us!" Abby grabbed her wrist and pulled her out of the limo the instant the driver opened their door.

Conner squeezed between them so he looked like the luckiest guy in Hollywood. Then he stuck an unlit cigarette in the side of his mouth.

Dozens of cameras clicked and flashed until Claire was convinced she'd be deaf and blind forever.

"Over here!" someone barked and pointed to the wide lens of his camera.

"Look here, please, Miss Lyons."

Claire had no idea who that was or how they knew her name.

"Abby, over here."

"Conner!"

"Claire! Conner! Abby! Over here!"

Claire tried to look at the right place and smile at the right time but couldn't fight the feeling that she was trapped inside a tornado, spinning and reeling out of control.

"You thinking what I'm thinking?" Abby murmured.

"Huh?" Claire asked, through her toothy smile.

"Yeah." Conner nodded. "Hold on, babygirls."

He tightened his grip so that the girls were mashed up against either side of his hard torso. In one swift move he thrust the girls onto the benchlike backseat of the limo. The paparazzi moved closer toward the car, flashing and clicking and calling their names.

"Incoming!" Conner shouted as he dove on top of the girls.

The driver slammed the door behind them and tore down La Cienega Boulevard, ignoring the photographers who were running alongside the car, begging them to stop.

"You can get off us now." Abby tickled Conner's ribs until he jumped back.

Claire sat up and smoothed her hair. "That was crazy."

"Wait until the movie comes out." Abby laughed.

Claire looked at the drivers in the cars beside them, wondering if one day they would know who she was and, more important, if she wanted them to. But that was too much to think about now. Her brain throbbed and her stomach was grumbling.

"Who wants In-N-Out burgers?" Conner licked his puffy lips.

"Only if you don't tell Rupert." Abby pinched her flat stomach.

"What's In-N-Out?" Claire asked.

Conner pulled off his blazer. Claire could see his bumpy ab muscles through his tight white tee. "Only the best burgers in the country."

"Yes!" She pulled off her boots and kicked up her feet.

"May I?" Conner pulled off Claire's sweaty gray J. Crew socks and tossed them out the sunroof. Then he began rubbing the soles of her feet with gentle determination. She could feel it all the way to the tips of her ears.

"Don't you two look cozy," Abby purred.

But Claire was too sleepy to answer. She just sat back and enjoyed getting her feet rubbed by "the teen dream." For the first time all day, cheating boyfriends and angry girlfriends were the furthest things from her mind.

Claire stepped out of the limo carrying her cowboy boots.

"Don't forget this, babygirl." Conner's tanned arm appeared through the open window swinging her phone.

"Thanks." She held out her palm and he let go.

"See you tomorrow!" Abby shouted as the limo continued out the circular driveway.

"Bye." Claire giggled. Her cheeks were tight from laughing.

"Rough night?" asked the doorman as she shuffled past him in her bare feet.

"No, but it will be." She thought of Massie and Alicia, who were probably in bed sharpening their nails so they could tear her apart for not calling them back.

The elevator opened before Claire pushed the button. As the doors closed, she turned on her phone. It lit up and vibrated. Five messages. Finally, when she reached the twenty-fifth floor, she took a deep breath and pressed play.

"Hey, Claire, it's me, Layne. So I have the full report and you're never gonna believe—

"Hey, sorry, I dropped the phone in a bowl of green Jell-O—Ew, Meena, stop that! . . . Anyway, the big story of the night is Derrington. He showed up wearing green shorts and no shirt. He wrote, 'I'm With Massie,' across his chest in purple Sharpie. The dean kicked him out as soon as he got here because he refused to cover up and— No WAY! . . . I love Shakira. . . . I have to dance to this one. . . . I'll call you right back."

"Noooo!" Claire punched her phone. If it hadn't been a gift, she would have hurled it against the wall.

"Me again, I just had a Cam sighting. And you'll never guess who he's with. Give up? Okay, I'll tell you. It's Todd. Your brother, who is covered in tattoos, by the way."

Claire jumped up and down, ignoring the couple a few feet away struggling with their key card.

"Word is, he had to bring a date so he asked your bro. The coach couldn't say no cuz of discrimination so they're dancing right now to Bubba Sparxxx. 'Kay, I gotta go practice. The dance contest is coming up and I so want that Chili's gift certificate. Wish me luck."

"Hey, superstar, it's me, Cam. And I wanted you to know I'm breaking up with you so I can start hanging out with Todd. He's a much better dancer."

Todd was giggling in the background while Cam was trying to hang up. She played his message four more times, then called her mother and told her she'd gotten home safely.

She put the key in the door, ready to face Massie and Alicia and whatever it was they had in store for her. She'd had the perfect night, and no matter how hard they tried, they would never be able to take that away from her.

The suite was dark and silent. And the bedroom doors were closed.

Just to be safe, Claire slept on the satin couch and tiptoed out the next morning before they woke up.

┌─────────────────────────────────────┐
│ LE BACCARAT HOTEL   │
│ CRYSTAL SLIPPER DINING ROOM   │
│ Monday, March 23rd   │
│ 5:00 A.M.   │
└─────────────────────────────────────┘

Massie dropped a crispy strip of bacon inside her purple Coach dog carrier when the waiters weren't looking. Bean sniffed it with her wet black nose, then gobbled it up.

"Make sure you don't get any on your outfit," she told her pug-slash-cohost for the day. Bean's pink puppy Uggs and green Polo minidress were sure to be a hit.

"Merri-Lee is going to love this idea!" Alicia pinched off a piece of her blueberry muffin.

"Ah-greed."

Ever since their disastrous first show, the girls had stayed up late, rehearsing and brainstorming new material. And it was paying off. So what if Hal thought they needed more celebrity interviews? What did he know? If he had any talent at all, he'd be in front of the camera, not behind it.

"Great news, dear!" Kendra called from the other side of the hotel's elegant dining room. Judi Lyons was with her, dressed in high-waisted capri pants and a rose-colored sweater set.

Massie pushed her sugar-free hot chocolate aside. "What are *they* doing up?"

"Morning, sunshine." Kendra air-kissed her daughter's cheek. "We just got off a conference call with Emma,

Rupert's darling assistant." She slid a wing chair over from a neighboring table and placed it between Massie and Alicia. Judi did the same.

Massie leaned forward. "What'd she say?"

"You and Alicia can share Claire's tutor." Kendra dangled a cup in the air. A waiter rushed over and filled it with coffee.

"And Claire doesn't mind one bit," Judi gushed.

Massie kicked Alicia under the table. Alicia kicked her back.

"You start tonight." Kendra tore open a packet of Splenda and dumped it in her coffee. "Thank heavens. I am so worried about you falling behind. But let's not think about that now."

Massie pushed her toast aside. Repeating the seventh grade was not an option. If she had to sit through another year of integers and fractions, she would tear out her hair extensions, wrap them around her neck, and hang herself from the chandelier.

Yap-yap-yap . . .

Yap-yap-yap . . .

"No barking," Kendra scolded her daughter's Coach bag.

"It's my phone." Massie flipped over her Razr. "Hello?"

"Sweetie, it's Calgary."

"Oh, hey, Calgary."

Alicia jumped up, forced her tiny butt onto Massie's chair, and pressed her ear against the phone.

"Listen, honey," she whispered. "There's been talk of replacing you."

Alicia grabbed Massie's wrist.

"What? Why?"

"You're not getting the goods," Calgary explained. "Claire is the only celeb you got us. Love the girl to death, but let's face it: She's not A-list."

Massie could have listened to her say those last three words all day.

"We need Abby and Conner and Rupert," Calgary insisted. "No more of your parking-lot tours, craft-service-table exposés, or searches for the 'best boy.' We need real celebrity dirt or . . . let's just say you have until Wednesday to turn the show around."

"What about—" Massie was about to ask Calgary her opinion on Bean cohosting but stopped herself. She hung up her phone and handed the Coach dog carrier to her mother.

"What's this?" Kendra asked.

Massie stood up from the table. "Change of plans."

She grabbed Alicia's arm and pulled her through the dining room.

"Ouch, let go," Alicia giggle-whined. "What's the rush?"

Dial L for Last Chance. Dial F for Fired. Dial WNBATSOFI-PAACWBMFTU for We'll Never Be Able to Show Our Faces in Public Again and Claire Will Be More Famous Than Us.

All of those would have been appropriate answers. But Massie said nothing. She had one hour to think of a new show idea. And needed all the time she could get.

"To the nearest pharmacy, please," Massie told her driver when they got in the Escalade.

"What do you need?" Alicia asked. "Are you sick?"

"No." Massie sat back and smirked. "But poor Claire is."

"Do you think that's why she's been sleeping on the couch lately?"

"Has she been?" Massie buckled her seat belt. "Funny. I didn't notice."

GELDING STUDIOS
MAKEUP TRAILER A
Monday, March 23rd
6:20 A.M.

"Okay, girls, I'm looking for one-word answers here." Lynn, the *Teen Vogue* reporter, flipped a page in her notebook and crossed her legs. "It's for an online feature we call 'Favorite Things.'"

"Ready." Abby snapped her fingers.

"Yeah, ready." Claire pulled a blond piece of hair out of her Silly Putty–colored lipstick, hoping the reporter would have the sense to know that she didn't normally look like a corpse.

They were seated in front of the mirror in makeup trailer A, wearing their Lakeview uniforms while Gina sponged and dabbed mounds of base on their faces so they'd look "natural" for the homeroom scene.

Since Abby was playing Suze, she got to wear blond hair extensions, rosy blush, glitter eyeliner, and tinted lip gloss. Claire's character, Molly, had dark under-eye circles and sallow skin. The short bangs, however, didn't need modification. Gina had decided they were perfectly dorky just the way they were.

"Here we go." Lynn plucked a pen out of the blond pile of curls on top of her head.

"Cool trick." Abby snapped twice.

"Thanks." She crossed her legs the other way, then became intensely serious. "Here we go. Favorite hobby."

"Photography," Claire answered.

"Jewelry design." Abby wiggled her fingers in front of the mirror so Lynn could see her collection.

"Did you make those?" she asked, pen at the ready.

"Mentally, yes. I designed them, then paid some dude to realify them."

Lynn scribbled.

"Next question. Favorite junk food."

"Mints." Abby shook her green ring. The tiny mints jingled.

Claire smiled to herself. "Gummy bears and worms."

"Lie!" Abby snapped once.

"What?" Claire was taken aback.

"Red Vines. You love Red Vines. That's why catering always puts them out on the table. For you!"

"Point." Claire borrowed Alicia's word. "Okay, Red Vines." She didn't want to argue in front of the reporter.

"And finally, the initials of your crush." Lynn tapped her pen against her teeth.

"That's easy." Claire beamed. "CF."

"Me too." Abby raised her eyebrows in a how-do-you-like-me-now-sort of way.

"Is it the same CF?" Lynn leaned closer. "Is there trouble on the set *again*?"

"No trouble here." Abby put her arm around Claire.

"Okay, then." Lynn stood and shook the girls' hands.

"The full interview will be in the June issue of *Teen Vogue*, but your 'favorite things' will be posted on our Web site by the end of the day."

As soon as Lynn left the makeup trailer, Abby turned to Claire. "So who's *your* CF?"

"Cam Fisher, my boyfriend." Claire knit her pencil-enhanced eyebrows. "You know that."

"Of course I do. I was just kidding."

"Who's yours?" Claire asked.

"Cam Fisher." Abby laughed. "When we wrap, I'm going to fly to Westchester and steal him from you." She threw her head back and giggled wildly.

Claire shifted in her seat.

"I'm kidding." Abby wiped her eyes.

"Nooooo." Gina rushed to her side. "Abby, you smudged!"

"It was an accistake," she insisted, then cranked up the volume on Gina's iPod. "Wooo-hoooo!" The starlet waved her arms and thrust her pelvis to Fall Out Boy's "A Little Less Sixteen Candles."

Claire started bopping in her seat, trying to dance the image of Abby lip-kissing Cam out of her mind—even though she had to have been *joking*. Right?

Next thing she knew, Gina was shaking her butt and Abby was smacking it. Riding to school with the Pretty Committee used to be the coolest way to start the day, but not anymore.

"Awesome! Conner *loves Dancing with the Stars*." Conner

stepped into the trailer and handed each of the girls a coffee. His black hair was spiked to perfection.

"What are you doing here?" Abby snapped. "My makeup isn't done!"

"I thought I'd brighten your day." He flipped a Marlboro Red in the air and caught it between his full lips.

"No smoking in here." Gina flicked a pink packet of Sweet'n Low.

"Relax, babygirl." He slid on a pair of aviators. "Conner doesn't light them." He kicked open the trailer door, lifted his sunglasses, and winked at Claire on his way out.

Her teeth started to chatter. She loved being around Conner and Abby. Not because they were famous or cool or beautiful or rich, but because they were full of quirks and made no attempt to hide them. They reminded her of Layne in that way. And she was grateful to have found them. If she hadn't, she would have been stuck watching the fun instead of taking part in it. Like she usually was.

Abby sighed. "I think he likes you."

"Who?"

"Conner!"

Claire blushed. "Yeah, right!" But she had secretly wondered the same thing herself. He was always flirting with her and making up excuses to be around them. Not that she'd ever do anything about it. She had lost Cam once and was not about to lose him again. So what if Conner was a gorgeous movie star? That shouldn't matter. And it didn't. No matter how much her clammy hands said it did.

"I'm serious." Abby turned to Claire.

Gina lifted the eyeliner pencil away from Abby's face and waited patiently for her to face forward again.

"What if he made a move on you?" she asked.

"Like he ever would." Claire blushed again.

"'Like he ever would,'" Abby repeated. "Let's just pretend. What would you do?"

"I'd remind him I have a boyfriend." Claire bit into a Red Vine.

Massie threw open the door of the trailer. "Morning!"

"Morning," Alicia chirped.

"Hey!" Claire was happy to see her old friends. Even though they had been distant lately, their familiar faces were comforting.

But Massie was all business. "We're going live in five minutes and we want to do the show from—"

"Get out!" Abby whipped her coffee at the door.

Claire gasped. The steaming cup missed Massie's head by a few inches.

"Ehmagawd!" Alicia squealed.

"You okay?" Claire raced to her side.

"Totally," Massie said, like she dodged burning liquid for a living.

"No one is allowed to see me without my makeup. No one! Do you know how much a naked face goes for in *Us Weekly*?"

"Believe me, Abby, the last thing I want is a shot of your face without makeup." Massie managed to stay calm, but Claire knew how hard this butt-kissing must be for her.

"If you want, I can show you where all the extras are," Claire offered. "There's this one guy who has been in sixty movies. And he has this story about the time he met—"

"Puh-lease, Kuh-laire." Massie rolled her eyes. "No one cares about the extras."

"Point." Alicia lifted her finger.

"Hey, that's Claire's word." Abby turned around in her chair and gave Alicia the stink-eye.

"*What?*" Alicia screeched.

Claire immediately lowered her head, knowing she would pay for that later.

"Outta here before I shove a pumpkin ball up your ass!" Abby yelled.

Claire burst out laughing. "What's a pumpkin ball?"

Abby cracked up. "I dunno." Tears rolled down her face. "It just came out."

The girls were in hysterics.

"Oh, wait." Abby spun around and faced the mirror. "Are these the girls you blew off the night we went to Boi?"

Claire sobered up immediately. "I didn't *forget* to invite them. I was trying to call—" She faced Massie. "I was trying to call you when—"

"That's when Conner took your phone, right?" Abby was still laughing. "The night I tagged the security guard with my underwear."

The memory of Abby whipping her thong out the limo window cracked Claire up all over again. She willed herself to stop but couldn't. Abby's "har-har-har"ing was contagious.

Massie's cheeks were red and her amber eyes flickered.

Abby wiped the tears from her eyes, then checked herself in the mirror. A silver band of glitter streaked across her cheek like a meteor shower.

"Abby, stop laughing!" Gina grabbed a handful of tissues. "Your mascara is running."

"Doesn't it sound like Conner likes Claire?" Abby asked, oblivious to Gina's frustration.

Claire silently begged her to stop. She had never seen Massie look so furious. Her cheeks were red, her eyes were all squinty, and her fists were clenched. "I seriously think he likes you," Abby continued.

"He doesn't, okay?" Claire's tone was flat.

"Well, it's not like he likes *me*," Abby announced. "That's for sure."

"I'm sure Cam would be happy to know you have a celebrity crush." Massie picked her cuticle.

Claire jumped out of her seat. "Please don't say anything to him. There's nothing going on, I swear."

Massie smirked.

Claire's hands suddenly felt icy.

"We're live in a minute thirty." Hal pounded on the trailer door.

"Come on, Abby," Massie pleaded. "Just a quick interview. We won't do a close-up."

Claire knew she could have pressed the issue and could have possibly convinced Abby to say yes. But she didn't. This fight had nothing to do with her, and it felt great not to be involved.

"Okay, if it will help you guys, I'd be happy to do it." Abby smiled.

"Yes!" Massie lifted her palm and high-fived Alicia.

"Really?" Claire breathed a sigh of relief. Finally, she had met someone who understood the true meaning of friendship.

Abby pulled away and shook her head. "Ha! How funny would it be if I was actually like that?"

"What?"

"I said, no cameras!" she growled. "And I meant it."

"Three minutes. That's all we need." Massie clasped her hands together. "Please! Our entire futures depend on it."

"Eighty seconds!" Hal announced.

"Kuh-laire, do something," Massie pleaded.

But Claire froze.

"Forget it." Alicia tugged Massie's red cashmere T-shirt. "We'll find something else to shoot."

"Like ourselves." Massie sighed.

"Sixty seconds." Hal stuck his head inside. "Do you girls have a plan?"

Massie suddenly lifted her head. "Yup. Let's go!"

"Thanks a lot," Alicia uttered as she followed her out.

"Wait!" Claire called.

But it was too late. They were gone.

Abby closed her eyes so Gina could get back to work. "I bet they're big losers back home."

Claire sighed. "You have no idea."

"Access denied." A bald security guard held out his arm and stopped Massie from entering Claire's trailer.

After everything she had just been through, there was no way some wannabe cop was going to stand in her way.

"Believe me, I don't *want* to go in there: I have more important things to do." She pointed to her cameraman. "So if you would take Claire's personal items and set them up for her in the bathroom, I'd really appreciate it." Massie handed him a plastic Rite-Aid bag.

He peeked inside, then quickly handed it back. "Make it fast."

"Thank you." Alicia clapped her hands.

"Fifteen seconds," the producer announced.

"Let's go." Massie led the way.

"Wait, no cameras," the security guard barked.

"You tell that to the millions of people watching *The Daily Grind*." Massie opened the door. "We're about to go live and I can't be in two places at once."

Massie prayed to Gawd the security guard would fall for her lame explanation, even though it made zero sense.

"*The Daily Grind*?" he asked. "Mother loves that show."

"I'll give you an autograph as soon as we're done." Massie winked. "For Mother."

He smiled and returned her wink.

The inside of the trailer was more chic than Massie had imagined. Sisal rugs covered most of the floor space, and the walls were adorned with vintage movie posters. A cream-colored couch lined one side and a desk and kitchenette lined the other.

"Eight seconds."

"Ehmagawd, here." Massie handed the bag to Alicia. "Do it, quick!"

"Why do I have to do it?"

"Because someone has to be on camera when the show starts."

"Why can't it be *me*?"

"In three . . ."

Massie shoved Alicia aside.

"Two . . . and . . ." The producer shook his finger.

"What's up, Merri-Lee? Massie Block here from the set of *Dial L for Loser*. Claire Lyons is in makeup and didn't want us to show the world what she looked like with a naked face. Can you blame her?" She giggled. "But she was nice enough to give us an exclusive on her trailer. You'd be surprised how much you can learn about a person by looking through their things."

"Look what I found," Alicia called. The camera whipped around to find her. She was pointing to a corkboard that hung above the glass desk. Textbooks and binders covered most of the surface, reminding Massie that she had a ton of ah-nnoying history homework to do after the show, thanks to Mrs. Mendel, her tutor.

"Claire has pictures of her friends all over the place," Alicia said to the camera.

There was a photo of Cam in his soccer uniform; Jay, Judi, and Todd in their family room; and several of the Pretty Committee, some of which had been taken at Lake Placid, but most of which showed the girls cracking up at Massie's Friday night sleepovers.

In the center of the collage was a shot of Claire with her arm around Massie. They were sitting on the steps of the Blocks' estate. Claire's striped scarf was wrapped around both of their necks, and they were giving each other bunny ears. It had been taken one month earlier, yet it seemed like a lifetime ago.

"Ew, look," Massie squealed. She pointed at the mess in Claire's bathroom. The camera zoomed in. "Let's talk trash!"

"G-ross!" Alicia ran into frame and put on her best I'm-so-disgusted face.

Massie knelt down and rummaged through the mess on the floor. "It appears as though our lead actress has been suffering from a bad case of nerves." She held up a pink bottle of Pepto-Bismol. "And judging from this big tube of Oxy, she also has some major zits."

"And bad breath." Alicia held up a bottle of Listerine.

"And a mustache." Massie held up a box of Jolene face bleach.

"And bladder-control issues." Alicia held up a package of Depends undergarments.

"And female baldness." Massie displayed a box of ladies' Rogaine.

"And dandruff." Alicia held up a bottle of Head & Shoulders.

"And athlete's foot." Massie sprayed some Desenex.

"And jock itch." Alicia burst out laughing as she threw a can of Cruex over her shoulder.

"The cool thing about 'talking trash'"—Massie made air quotes—"is that you get information about someone that they would never give you in a regular interview."

"You can say that again." Alicia threw a box of super-plus-size tampons across the floor.

All of a sudden, there was a loud knock. Had the security guard finally realized he had been tricked? Had he gotten Claire? Were they about to get shut down?

"Who is it?" Massie asked. "This is what live TV is all about, right? You never know what's going to happen," she explained to her viewers.

"Claire, it's Conner."

Massie and Alicia grabbed the handle at the same time and threw open the door.

"Velvet?"

"Rooty!" Massie pulled the actor inside the trailer like they had been BFFs for years. Maybe a rumor would spread that they were a couple.

"Hey, Conner." Alicia tilted her head to one side and batted her long lashes.

"Hey, babygirls, is Claire here? We're supposed to rehearse the homeroom scene." He scanned the trailer. "Hey, what's with the cameras?"

"We're live on *The Daily Grind*," Massie explained.

The producer started "whoop-dee-do"-ing his finger, which meant it was time for them to wrap it up.

"Before we go . . ." Massie spoke as fast as she could. "Tell the people at home what you do to prepare for your role as the ah-dorable Brad Douglas."

"This is an easy one for me because Brad is a good-looking, popular guy." Conner pulled a toothpick out of his back pocket and stuck it in his mouth. "He is tough on the outside and a sweetheart on the inside." He flipped the toothpick with his tongue. "So, all Conner has to do is show up and his work is done."

"One last thing." Alicia ignored the producer's swirling finger. "Are those new Conner Foley jeans? I notice the stitching is white on this pair."

Massie hated that Alicia had noticed that before she did.

"Good eye, babygirl." Conner spun around and shook his butt for the camera. It was a total Derrington move and Massie suddenly found herself missing him. Hopefully, Kristen and Dylan were keeping close tabs on him.

"Conner gets a new pair of custom-made CF jeans every time he stars in a new movie," he explained. "I have nineteen pairs so far."

Hal twirled his finger so quickly, he seemed ready for liftoff.

Massie took the cue. "Thank you, Rooty—I mean, Conner." She turned to the camera. "Well, that's all for today. I'll be back tomorrow with more 'trash talk' and interviews from the set of *Dial L for Loser*. Until then, I'm Massie Block—"

"And I'm Alicia Rivera, and we heart you."

"Aaaand we're out!" Hal announced. "Great show, everyone."

"Thanks for the interview, Rooty," Massie cooed.

"The pleasure was mine, Velvet." Conner took the toothpick out of his mouth and crushed it. He was about to toss it in the garbage can but suddenly stopped himself. "Who blew up the pharmacy?"

Massie was tempted to tell him the truth. But what if he thought they were mean? Or worse, what if word got back to Merri-Lee? She'd know the segment had been faked and they'd be fired. Unfortunately, Conner would have to believe Claire was a nervous, stinky, hairy, incontinent, balding, flaky, itchy mess. Just like the rest of America would.

Massie and Alicia were celebrating their Conner interview with toasted bagels and sugar-free hot chocolates. Neither had mentioned the piece they did on Claire, which Massie took as a good sign. Maybe it wasn't such a big deal after all.

Yap-yap-yap . . .

Yap-yap-yap . . .

"Hey, Dyl," she answered with a genuine smile.

"Heyyyy!" Alicia shouted. She pressed her ear against Massie's phone and listened in.

"Hold on while I get Kristen."

" 'Kay," Massie and Alicia said at the same time.

"Apple-C!" they shouted, then high-fived each other.

Two guys covered in paint at a nearby table shot them dirty looks, then returned to their large coffees and newspapers.

"Whoever said making movies was glamorous ahbviously never saw the behind-the-scenes people," Massie whispered.

"Point." Alicia held up her finger, then quickly lowered it. "Didn't mean to steal *Claire's* word."

Massie suddenly felt less guilty about what they had done. Claire was hardly innocent. She'd practically stolen their identities, then refused to help them get an Abby interview. The more she thought about it, the more she realized Claire deserved exactly what she got.

"Hey." Kristen was suddenly on the line.

"Did you guys see the show today?" Alicia bit her bottom lip.

"Given!" Kristen answered.

"Everyone is talking about it," Dylan gushed.

Massie pushed her bagel aside. "How dead are we?"

"Dead?" Dylan sounded shocked. "Puh-lease, you got an exclusive with Conner. Not even *Entertainment Tonight* did that."

"Really?" She popped a sesame seed in her mouth. "Did your mom like it?"

"Loved it!" Dylan insisted. "And she can't believe Claire let you shoot that stuff in her trailer. No one can." She paused. "By the way, is she copying my bran diet?"

"Maybe." Massie couldn't bring herself to tell them what she had done.

"Ehmagawd, and get this," Kristen cried. "I heard a few girls at OCD bought the same black striped Keds Claire wore in her interview the other day. She's, like, a real star. It's so weird."

"I know, aren't you glad we let her in the Pretty Committee?" Dylan added. "Everyone will be so jealous that we're BFFs with an actress."

"Puh-lease." Massie punched her bagel. "No one's a real star until they're in *US Weekly*."

"How's Josh?" Alicia chewed her coffee stirrer into a gnarled clump.

"Ah-dorable." Kristen chuckled. "He wrote this comic book called *Bleacher Creatures*. It's about me and Dylan, only we're these sexy soccer fans who live under the bleachers and—"

"Am I in it?" Alicia's eyes widened.

"Uh . . ." Dylan giggled nervously. "Not yet. But that doesn't mean—"

"What about the protests?"

"Da Crew has disbanded," Kristen explained. "Apparently, Strawberry wanted to join Layne's protests."

"And a vote for Layne is a vote for Claire," Dylan added. "Which is good for us."

Massie couldn't believe Claire had become so important to the cause.

"What about the Country Club?" Massie asked.

"No word yet, but I'm sure once they hear about your Conner interview they'll be back with us," Kristen said.

"Any news about anyone else?" Massie couldn't bring herself to ask specifically about Derrington. She didn't want to sound like Claire, whose obsession with Cam made her look so desperate and needy.

"The spring clothes are starting to go on display, and there are a lot of bold colors and ruffles this season," Dylan reported. "Oh, and wedge heels are gonna be big."

"And Norma—the pedicure lady you love?—is on maternity leave," Kristen said.

"Anything else?" Massie pressed. "You know, about the guys or anything?"

"Oh, a time has been set for the board meeting. Six o'clock on April third."

"Who knows?" Massie examined the ends of her extensions. "We may not go back. You know, if this whole reporting thing keeps going well."

"Point," Alicia said.

"So there's nothing else, about the guys, the soccer games, or Briarwood?"

"We're meeting the team for pizza after practice tonight." Kristen sounded a little too excited. "Josh wants to show us a few new *Bleacher Creatures* sketches."

"Tell him to put us in it," Alicia piped up.

"We'll try," Dylan said, as if she had just been asked to stop eating for a month.

"Have fun." Massie tried to sound sincere. "Tell the guys we say hi."

"'Kay, call us later."

"Can't." Massie winked at Alicia. "We have plans with Conner and, well, you know how it is."

"There he is now. We gotta go." Alicia closed her phone.

Massie looked up, in case she had been serious. But Conner wasn't there. Claire was.

Her eyes were red and her skin was blotchy. Abby's arm was around her shoulders, steering her toward an empty table. As they passed by Massie and Alicia, Abby tightened her grip.

"Did they see us?" Massie asked.

"Hard to say. Should we go over and say hi? You know, to see if they're mad?"

Massie wasn't sure *what* to do. What if Claire told her off in front of Abby, her hair muse? She'd never recover. Gawd, this whole thing was so ah-nnoying! If Abby only knew how many people worshipped Massie back home. She'd drop Claire faster than an itchy mohair sweater.

But if Massie ignored them, she'd never know if she and Alica had gotten away with their 'trash talk' segment. And the suspense was killing her.

"Let's go." Massie grabbed Alicia's thin wrist. There was no reason to be nervous. It was Kuh-laire, after all: the girl who'd worn Keds and overalls on her first day of school. The girl with lopsided bangs. The girl who ate candy for break-fast. The girl who thought cameras were cooler than credit cards. Puh-lease! If Claire said *anything* to Massie, it had better be "Thank you for giving me life."

Then, suddenly, Rupert appeared.

"Brilliant!" he shouted as he raced to Claire's table. "I haven't seen tears like that since Dakota Fanning's perform-ance in *Uptown Girls*. Truly remarkable."

"Conner thought you were great too." The actor mussed Claire's hair as he joined them.

"Thanks." She lowered her eyes.

Massie felt like she was watching a play, so close to the action, yet completely removed at the same time. She sighed, hoping someone would acknowledge her, but they were too busy fawning all over Dakota Lyons.

Conner put his thumb under Claire's chin and lifted her face.

"Babygirl, can I ask you a question?"

Claire nodded.

"Where do you get your motivation? You know, to cry like that? Conner has a hard time with tears." He stuck his finger through the Mercedes logo on his key chain and began twirling his keys. "What's your secret?"

Claire pointed at Massie and Alicia. "Them."

Alicia gasped.

Massie's heart rate shot up. She was short of breath and her lips were screaming for gloss. Everyone was staring at her, but not in a good way.

Conner turned to face Massie. "Velvet, do you think you could help *me*?"

Massie opened her mouth, but Abby's voice came out.

"Of course she can help you. All she has to do is ruin your life like she ruinified Claire's and you'll cry buckets."

"Puh-lease." Massie used her best stop-being-so-dramatic voice. Maybe if she acted like this whole thing was no big deal they'd believe it. "There's no such thing as bad press."

"No, just bad friends." Claire glared, her blue eyes filled with a mix of hate and heartbreak.

"No wonder you got this part." Massie cleared her throat. "You're a total drama queen." She stormed off, grateful for the sound of Alicia's Michael Kors cork wedges shuffling behind her.

"Wait up," she heard someone call.

It was Conner.

She quickly licked her lips before turning around, hoping her saliva would pass as gloss.

"I would love you to show me how to tap into my emotions." Conner pouted his Red Bull–colored lips.

"Uh, okay." Massie pretended to know exactly how to do that. "No prob."

"I can help too," Alicia offered.

"Of course you can, babygirl." He half smiled. "How about you two come swimming at my place in Malibu this Saturday?"

"Done," Alicia answered a little too quickly.

"Done," Massie confirmed, the cells in her body bouncing like millions of little pearls on a marble floor.

And to think she'd been worried about Claire ruining her social life.

Im-possible!

CURRENT STATE OF THE UNION

IN	OUT
Trash talk	Straight talk
Saturday afternoon pool parties	Friday night sleepovers
Conner Foley	Derrington

Abby snapped twice. "Lyons, you're in!"

"Huh?" Claire plopped down on Conner's red velvet couch beside her. Never in a million years did she ever think she'd be plopping on Conner's *anything* with Abby Boyd.

"Remember the photographer who snapped our picture when we walked out of Coffee Bean & Tea Leaf?"

"Yeah." Claire's heart started to race, like it knew what was coming before she did.

"Well, his shot made it into *US Weekly*." Abby beamed. "Look! I scored an advance layout copy. It'll be on stands next week."

"Let Conner see." He ripped the magazine out of Abby's hands and pulled off his silver Dior wraparounds. "Man, that's a good one!"

Abby stuck her tongue out at him in a ha-ha-too-bad-you're-not-as-cool-as-me sort of way.

"Let me see." Claire reached for the magazine, but Conner pulled it even farther away.

"I can't believe it." He was staring at the picture, dumb-founded. "All the bases are covered. Your coffees are in to-go cups, which says, 'I'm very busy. No time to eat.' You're laughing, which says, 'We are successful and happy.' And you both look skinny, which says, 'I'm skinny!'" He held up his palm. "Nice going!"

The girls double-high-fived him.

Claire grabbed the magazine. "Wow," was all she could say. Conner was right. It was a great shot. She and Abby were wearing matching peach-colored Juicy sweat suits (a gift from the designers) and were cracking up outside the coffee shop. They looked like true BFFs.

"You can thank me later." Abby beamed.

"What do you mean?" Claire didn't want to sound rude or ungrateful but *huh*?

"What do I mean?" she teased. "I asked one of my paparazzi contacts to take it. I knew it would piss off your loser friends." She looked proud, almost heroic. Like she had just rescued a baby from the jaws of a hungry shark.

Claire bit her thumbnail.

"Don'tcha love press wars?" Abby opened her green ring, dipped her pinky inside, then dabbed behind her ears. The light floral aroma of lilies of the valley filled the room.

Claire knit her blond brows.

"Everyone out here does it, right, Conner?" Abby seemed annoyed that Conner was reading the ingredients on the back of his protein shake instead of listening to her.

"Right, babygirl," he said to a can of cookies-and-cream-flavored Muscle Milk.

"We fight using photographs," she explained. "Like, if I want to get a guy jealous, I'll have one of my contacts take a shot of me with some hot newcomer. And if he wants to get me back, he'll have a shot taken of him with *two* hot newcomers."

"Kind of like that shot of you hugging that skinny model dude from *8th & Ocean*."

Abby kicked the stack of boxes by the door marked HUGO BOSS and CF JEANS.

"Or that picture of you draped all over that redheaded snowboarder?"

"Gabor doesn't have red hair!"

"The other one, you know, the Flying Tomato guy."

Abby turned away again.

"Seriously?" Claire wondered how many of the countless celebrity photos she and Massie had pored over were staged. Then she flashed back to the shots of her, Conner, and Abby outside Boi.

A wave of terror washed over her. Was she the only "real" person on the planet? The only one who played by the rules? The only one who believed in honesty and truth? Maybe it would have been better if she had been born evil. At least then duplicitous behavior wouldn't come as such a shock.

"So, Abby, you were *pretending* to be my friend?" Claire knew she sounded pathetic but was too disappointed to care. "And Conner, you were pretending to date us?"

Abby snapped once. "Of course not. That's crazyotic. We *are* friends. Best friends." She hugged Claire.

"And Conner *is* dating both of you." He winked, then cracked open his Muscle Milk and stuffed it in a brown paper bag. "Hey, Claire, I think they're taping an episode of

Emotionally Unstable Girl next door. Maybe you should audition."

She burst out laughing. "Maybe you should watch." She threw a pillow at him. "It might help you tap into your *tears* and *emotions*."

Abby burst out laughing. "Yeah, what was up with *that*?"

"What?" He couldn't help smiling at himself. "Those *Daily Grind* girls were cute."

Claire rolled her eyes. For once couldn't someone think they were ugly?

"I invited them to my house on Saturday." Conner tilted his head back and took a long swig from the bag. "We're having a pool party."

Abby's expression hardened. "Which one do you like?"

"Yeah, which one?" Claire's stomach lurched. No matter what he said, it would be the wrong answer. Conner was *hers*.

"Dunno yet." He crushed the tin can in his hands and tossed it in the trash. "Depends on which one looks hotter in a bathing suit."

"Ew!" Claire heard herself say.

"Perv!" Abby knocked the back of his head.

"What?" Conner widened his olive-green eyes. "I have a reputation to uphold." He grabbed the crumpled *US Weekly* off the couch and turned to the front of the magazine. "Look."

Abby grabbed it out of his hands and read the caption aloud: 'Conner Foley with sexy middle-school dropouts Alice and Moosie.' She turned to Claire. "Aren't these your ex-friends?"

"What?"

She handed her the magazine.

When Claire saw the picture of Massie and Alicia cruising the Gelding lot in a golf cart driven by Conner, she almost barfed.

"How great is that shot?" He punched the air. "They look like models. And the fact that they're dropouts? Perfect for my bad-boy image."

Claire's first instinct was to speed dial the girls and tell them they were being taken advantage of. What if Derrington and Josh saw this? Or Principal Burns? She'd never let them back into OCD. If Claire took the limo, she could be back at the hotel in twenty minutes. They could meet up at the restaurant, talk about how pathetic Conner was, then come up with a revenge plan.

Claire sat back down on the couch. After all, there was no such thing as bad press. Right, Moosie?

"Thank Gawd for spray tans." Massie beamed after checking her reflection in the brass knocker on Conner's front door. "Rate me?"

"Nine-eight." Alicia licked her lips. "Me?"

"Same," Massie lied. Her purple eyelet Betsey Johnson halter dress, white ankle socks, and BCBG wedges were way more eye-catching than Alicia's white, toga-inspired sarong and gold lace-up sandals.

"Rate Bean." Massie adjusted the pug's pink frilly bikini.

"Ten." Alicia giggled. "Now ring the bell." She squirmed like she was holding in a pee.

Of course Alicia had gotten a spray tan too. And of course she'd used her diffuser that morning. So her black hair was perfectly wavy and frizz-free, despite the unforgiving salt air. Hopefully, Conner would be so taken by Massie's charm and confidence that he wouldn't notice Alicia and the whole beautiful Greek goddess thing she was working.

"Ring it!" Alicia looked over her shoulder. "He probably has a ton of security cameras, and if he sees us standing here like—"

Massie rang the bell. Twice.

Suddenly, she felt guilty about Derrington. What if he knew she had gone shopping and tanning for another guy?

"Who is it?" a woman asked over the intercom.

Bean barked once. Massie leaned in to the white box at the side of the door and pushed the button. "Massie Block. Conner invited me."

"And Alicia Rivera." Alicia rolled her eyes. "He invited me too."

"Oops. Sorry 'bout that."

"Welcome. I'm Estelle." A short, gray-haired lady with a rolling pin and a kind smile invited them in. "Conner is expecting you. He's out by the pool."

"Thanks." Massie tried not to look impressed by the high ceilings, the skylights, or the back wall that rolled up like a garage door and opened onto the pool. Her eyes grazed past the ginormous flat-screen TV that was mounted above the stone fireplace. And she did her best not to stare at the gray cashmere couch that hung from chains like a swing. It was best to let Estelle think she saw that sort of thing all the time.

"I just made a fresh batch of protein-enriched quinoa muffins. Would you like me to bring some outside once they've cooled?"

"Um, no thanks," Alicia smirked.

Massie bit her bottom lip to avoid laughing in the maid's face. "We'll just head out back, if that's okay."

"Of course." Estelle smoothed her black uniform. "Refreshments are on the bar. If you need something special, just give me a ring." She shook an imaginary bell, then returned to the kitchen.

The girls followed the haunting sound of James Blunt's old hit, "You're Beautiful," through the heavily air-conditioned living room and out to the pool. Massie imagined Conner singing that song to her during an impromptu night of celebrity karaoke and felt that tiny tingle again behind her belly button.

"Over here, babygirls." Conner wiggled his fingers as he drifted by on a silver raft. His oil-slicked six-pack glistened in the afternoon sun, and Massie thought of a thousand reasons why she should feel guilty about Derrington. Nine hundred and ninety-nine had to do with Conner's deep red board shorts and how ah-mazing they looked on him.

"Hey," Massie and Alicia said at the same time. "Apple-C!" they shouted, a little louder than usual.

Conner chuckled as he brought a bottle of root beer to his lips.

Massie lowered herself as gracefully as she could and un-fastened Bean's black-and-gold Chanel leash. The puppy shot toward the pool like a hairy cannonball and jumped in. Conner scooped her up and held her against his chiseled stomach.

After another sip of root beer, he placed the brown bottle in the raft's cup holder and sat up. Bean was still in his tanned arms. "Why don't you go change into your bathing suits. The cuh-ban-ya is all yours."

"Ehmagawd, are you Spanish?" Alicia beamed.

Here we go, Massie thought. Did she honestly think

Conner would be impressed just because her mother had a different passport?

"No one in America ever pronounces *cabaña* properly. It's so ah-nnoying," Alicia continued.

"I'm not Spanish per se, but I was in Barcelona for two nights doing a press junket." Conner removed his Dior wrap-arounds. "Why, are you?" He lifted Bean off his lap and plopped her back in the water. "It *would* explain your—dare I say *exotic*—charms."

"Let's go change." Massie grabbed Alicia's arm and they ran past the edge of the pool.

A stinging blast of air-conditioning welcomed the girls to the cabaña.

"Not bad." Massie stood in front of the mirrored wall.

"I know," Alicia agreed. "I love the whole mirrors-instead-of-wallpaper thing."

"No, I meant my outfit." Massie admired herself. "But the decorating is pretty cool too."

A freshly vacuumed rug gave the glorified dressing room a touch of elegance, while the nautical blue couches and conch lamps were charming reminders that the beach was a few feet away.

"How many gossip points do I get for finding *these*?" Alicia waved a pair of Conner's CF jeans like a flag.

"Ehmagawd, where—"

"They were hanging over the sauna door."

"Ew, do you think they smell like butt?" Massie crinkled her perfect ski-slope nose.

Alicia sniffed them.

"Ew!" Massie shouted.

"Aahhhhhhh!" Alicia squirmed, then whipped the jeans onto the carpet.

"Ew! They smell?"

"No. I mean, I don't think so." Alicia's expression was somewhere between laughing and crying. "But they *could* have."

"In that case . . ." Massie opened her metallic Juicy Couture tote and stuffed the jeans inside.

"What are you *doing*?" Alicia was practically bug-eyed.

"Proving that we were here." She made it sound like the most logical thing ever.

"Point!" Alicia lifted her finger. "But wait." She lowered it. "What if he catches you?"

"Puh-lease, he probably has a million pairs. He won't even notice they're gone."

"Point!"

The girls spent the next eleven minutes trying on different bathing suits and rating each other. Finally, Massie decided on her zebra-print bikini, while Alicia settled for a plain black one-piece. It wasn't her favorite, but it didn't make her boobs look quite as heaving as the others. And Massie wasn't about to argue. The more Alicia covered up, the less Conner would notice her.

"So, are you gonna go for him?" She turned to the side and examined her cleavage profile. "Because if not, I will. Josh and I haven't even kissed yet, so—"

Massie tied the string on her barely-there bottoms. "I think we should let Conner go for *us*. You know, let *him* decide. The last thing I want to do is compete with you. Ah-greed?"

"Ah-greed."

After a quick application of vanilla-cupcake-flavored Glossip Girl, Massie side-braided her long hair and led the way back out to the pool.

"Mercy." The actor ran a wet hand through his glistening black hair. "Conner likes what he sees."

Massie sucked in her already flat stomach, turned ever-so-slightly to the side, and lightly joined her index fingers to her thumbs. It was a pose she secretly referred to as the Red Carpet.

Yap-yap-yap . . .

Yap-yap-yap . . .

She made a move for her phone but then realized the barking was coming from Bean. Conner had deposited her on the edge of the pool, and she was racing toward the rustling bushes that separated the property from the beach.

"Does Estelle do gardening too?" Massie tried to imagine her own maid, Inez, trimming the hedges. But it was impossible. Inez was never more than twenty feet away from the kitchen.

"No, why?" Conner lifted himself out of the pool and dried his hair with a black CF towel, leaving the sun to take care of the beading water droplets on the rest of his body.

"Looks like there's someone in your bushes."

"Probably a couple of tourists with a star map." Conner scratched the back of his head and gazed pensively toward the horizon. He might as well have been shooting another Hugo Boss ad. "It's the price of fame, Velvet."

Massie felt like a soaring balloon every time Conner called her that. Poor Alicia. She didn't have a chance.

"Would one of you babygirls like to be Conner's date for the wrap party next Friday night?"

"I would!"

"Apple-C!"

"I would!"

"Double apple-C!"

"I would!"

"Triple apple-C!"

"Hold on," he snickered. "Let's have a race! The first one to the end of the pool and back wins."

"Done!" Massie couldn't believe her luck. Alicia was genetically incapable of speed.

Hmmmm, what does one wear to a wrap party?

"Okay, then." Conner motioned for them to join him by the edge of the pool. "On your marks, get se—"

Splash!

Alicia did a stride jump into the water and took off. Her aversion to quickness must have been restricted to land sports, because she was hauling butt.

"Cheater!" Massie jumped in. Her zebra-striped top was sliding off and her bottoms were heading due north but she kept going. There was no way Alicia was going to beat her.

Left arm, right arm, turn to the side and breathe. Left arm, right arm, turn to the side and breathe. Left arm, right arm, turn to the side and breathe. Left arm, right arm, turn to the side and breathe. . . .

Bean was running along the edge of the pool, cheering her owner on until finally, Massie caught up. As she passed, she gave Alicia's hair a quick tug, letting her know she was no longer in the lead.

"Ouch!" Alicia shouted. She grabbed onto Massie's foot and yanked her back.

"Let go, cheater!" She kicked, doubling back and snapping the thick strap on Alicia's one-piece.

"Gawd, how desperate are you?" Alicia jumped on her back and held on tight.

"Get off me, pumpkin eater!"

"I am not a cheater!"

"You are!" Massie tried spinning, hoping to shake Alicia off. But she was sticking to her like waterproof mascara.

"I slipped."

"Well, *slip* on this!" Massie grabbed Conner's silver raft and slammed it down on Alicia's head until she lost her balance and fell off.

Someone was clapping. "Looks like a tie to me." Conner had two CF towels draped over his defined rotator cuffs.

"Then who gets to go to the wrap party?" Alicia asked in a high-pitched squeak.

"Both of you." He smiled.

Massie and Alicia glanced at each other and burst out

laughing. And just like that they were BFFs again. But that didn't mean Massie had to tell Alicia about the giant snot string dangling from her left nostril. Did it?

Bean started barking again.

"Sounds like the star-mappers are back." Alicia climbed up the pool ladder and pulled one of the towels from Conner's shoulder. She covered herself immediately.

The actor quickly spritzed himself with Hawaiian Tropic SPF 2. "Conner better check it out."

The instant he was gone, Massie pinched her bikini bottoms and pulled them out of her butt crack. Much better!

"Who's thirsty?" Estelle appeared with three glasses of mango juice.

The girls wasted no time lifting the tall glasses off her silver tray.

"Thanks," they said.

"My pleasure." She smiled. "I'm just so pleased my son has been hanging out with *nice* girls lately."

"Your *son*?" Alicia asked. "You mean you're not his—"

Massie cut her off. "Nice girls *lately*?"

Estelle nodded. "His girlfriend, Abby, had dinner with us last night."

"*Girlfriend?*"

"Apple-C!"

"Oh yes." Estelle dabbed her sweaty brow with a CF napkin. "They have been an item for almost three weeks. But they're always bickering." She quickly covered her mouth with her hand. "Ooopsie. You won't tell, right? I mean, they've been trying so hard to keep it from the press."

"No need to worry about *us*, Estelle." Massie tried to suppress her grin. "We *never* gossip."

"Never." Alicia shook her head.

"I knew you seemed like nice girls."

"Thank you." Massie smiled. "We try."

```
┌─────────────────────────────────────────┐
│            GELDING STUDIOS               │
│       LAKEVIEW MIDDLE SCHOOL SET         │
│              DETENTION                   │
│         Monday, March 30th               │
│              3:00 P.M.                    │
└─────────────────────────────────────────┘
```

Conner's mouth was so close to Claire's face, she could feel his warm breath on her cheek.

"There's an attraction between us that can't be denied." He leaned a tiny bit closer.

"Would you be saying that if I was still a nobody?" Claire looked him straight in the eye.

"Of course I would," he whispered. "True love doesn't discriminate."

Claire's pulse quickened. Her palms became clammy and her insides bunched up. *This is it,* she thought. *He's about to kiss me.*

All of a sudden she saw Cam's face. His blue eye and green eye filled with tears as Conner inched toward her trembling lips. How could she cheat on him again? Kissing Josh was one thing, a reaction to the pain Claire had felt when she thought Cam left her for Alicia's cousin Nina. But Conner Foley? The teen dream? Cam would *never* understand. Claire turned her head slightly to the side, to create a bit of space between their mouths while she thought this through.

"*Cut!*" Rupert shouted.

Massie and Alicia giggled, like they had every other time Rupert called "cut" because Claire messed up. She hated having them on set, especially during such an awkward scene. But they were Conner's guests. And he'd insisted they stay.

"Sweet-haht, what ah you doing?" Rupert paced the classroom set. He tried to sound patient, but to his credit, they had rehearsed the "first kiss" scene fourteen times, and Claire still wasn't getting it.

"Afta Brad says, 'True love doesn't discriminate,' yoh supposed to lean in so he can kiss you. You cahn't keep turning away." He unwrapped a stick of Big Red and jammed it in his mouth. Then he crumpled the wrapper in his fist and whipped it onto the ground.

"Sorry." Claire lowered her head. Tears blurred her vision, making her Lakeview Middle School skirt look like a plaid puddle. She knew making out with a gorgeous actor wasn't cheating if it was a scene in a movie. But still, it felt wrong.

"We have to staht rolling soon." Rupert ripped open four packets of sugar and dumped them in his tiny espresso cup. "So will you please focus?"

Massie and Alicia giggled again. Claire shot them a dirty look, which made them giggle even more.

"I'm ready!" Claire took a quick nibble out of her second-to-last gummy worm and forced it down her throat.

"Very well." Rupert sighed. "We're gonnah try this again. Everyone back to one, let's take it from 'Theh's an attraction.'" He cleared his throat. "And . . . action!"

"There's an attraction between us that can't be denied." Conner shifted in his seat to face her.

Claire gazed into his olive-green eyes. "Would you be saying that if I was still a nobody?" She turned to meet him, their knees touching ever so slightly.

"Of course I would," he whispered. "True love doesn't discriminate."

Claire took a deep breath, leaned forward, and jammed her mouth against his face. His lips didn't move at first. But once he realized she was going for it, he gripped the sides of her face and forced his tongue into her mouth. Her cheeks burned. Could Conner tell she was a tongue-virgin? She did her best to follow his lead. And before long, Claire was fully at ease, fully at one with Conner, and fully into it.

"Somebody stop her before she swallowcates his jaw!" Abby snapped her fingers frantically.

"Aaaand cut!" Rupert shouted. Claire could hear him smiling.

"Mercy." Conner touched his lips. "Nice going, babygirl."

"Thanks." She grinned.

"Brilliant, dahhh-ling!" Rupert rubbed the top of her head. "I knew you could do it."

"Do *what*?" Abby twisted off her mini-mint-filled ring and dumped them all in her mouth. "Act like a porn star?"

Massie and Alicia high-fived her like they were lifelong BFFs.

"She was wondaful," Rupert insisted.

"'She was wonderful,'" Abby mocked. "Molly would *never* kiss like that. She has no experience."

Despite the criticism, Claire welled with pride. Abby thought she was a good kisser!

"I'm just saying," the actress continued, "before Molly got a makeover from *my* character, she was a major loser. And even though she got a cool haircut and new clothes, she still has loser in her blood. And no loser would be *that* aggressive."

Claire clenched her jaw. How many more times was Abby going to remind everyone that she was playing a loser?

"It worked for Conner." The actor's cheeks were still flushed.

Abby marched over to him. "You know what else will work for Conner?" she snapped. "A Cup O' Noodles up your butt!"

"What does that *mean*?" he asked, an endearing smile on his face.

"I dunno." She shrugged. "It just came out."

Their eyes met and they snickered like giddy schoolgirls.

"Listen." Abby put her arm around Claire's shoulders. "I don't mean to sound all crictictatious." She gave her a reassuring squeeze. "I just want to do what's best for *our* movie. And I don't see your character being that, well, slutty. So maybe you can tone it down a bit."

"Uh, okay." Claire wasn't about to debate acting with Abby Boyd.

"We're ready to roll on this," Rupert announced. "I need all cameras. Now!"

Seconds later, the set was bustling with crew members hauling their gear and getting it into position.

Gina appeared at Claire's side with a bag of makeup.

"Uh, I need to make a quick call." She tried to sound harried so Gina would think it was an emergency. It was a Massie technique she'd picked up when the girls first met. "Be right back."

Stella was standing on the edge of the set scheduling interviews for her. "Here you go." She handed Claire her phone as if reading her mind.

"How did you know—"

"It's my job," Stella answered.

"Thanks." Claire still had a hard time believing Stella was there to take care of her every need. But as long as she was, there was no harm in asking for a favor, right?

"Stella, see those two girls by the coffee cart?" She pointed to Massie and Alicia.

"Conner's guests?"

"Yeah." She leaned in and whispered, "Would you mind having them removed from the set? They are ruining my focus." She felt bad, but acting was hard enough without Massie and Alicia cackling every time she messed up.

"Not a problem." Stella turned on the heels of her snakeskin stilettos and hurried toward the girls.

Claire crouched behind a massive klieg light and watched Stella do her dirty work. Whatever she said had Massie stomping her feet and Alicia craning to find Conner. Stella pointed to the exit, but the girls turned their backs to her. Finally, a stocky man in a mustard-colored SECURITY tee hauled them off the set. The instant they were gone, Claire exhaled. A weight had been lifted. But there was still one more thing crushing her. And it had Cam's name on it.

While the crew finished setting up, Claire hit speed dial number one, then lifted the red, shimmering phone to her ear. She was overflowing with guilt about the Conner kiss and needed to speak to Cam before she did it again.

Please answer. Please answer. Please an—

Someone picked up the phone but no one spoke.

"Cam?" She giggled. "Are you there? It's Claire."

Silence.

"Cam? Hello?" She checked the screen on her phone to make sure she'd dialed right. Maybe the signal was bad. "If you can hear me, don't go anywhere. I'll call you right back." She stuffed the rest of her second-to-last gummy worm in her mouth.

"I can hear you."

Claire's insides warmed from the sound of his voice. "Hey, it's me. I have a few minutes so I thought I'd call and say hey."

"Hey." His voice was flat.

"Hey." She knit her eyebrows. "Is everything okay? Were you sleeping?"

"No."

"Oh." She could hear herself breathing. "I'm eating a gummy worm right now."

"Really?" He sounded bored. "I thought your favorite snack food was Red Vines."

"Huh?" Her heart started thumping.

"I saw your *Teen Vogue* interview online."

"Oh, that." Claire tried to sound casual. Why had she ever listened to Abby? "I said gummy bears at first but then—"

"And you said your crush was CF."

"Yup," Claire confirmed with pride.

"Conner Foley?"

"What? No!" Her sadness was starting to grow teeth. "Obviously CF is you!"

"Is that why you were just making out with him?"

"What?" She looked around the studio. Had he shown up to surprise her?

"Massie sent a picture to my phone of you making out with him."

Claire lowered her head between her knees to keep from passing out. Was the 'trash talk' segment not mean enough? Was this *still* payback for having her off the set or leftover jealousy about the movie? Either way, it was beyond evil, even for Massie Block. "Cam, that was a scene from the movie."

"Then where were the cameras?" His voice shook.

"It was a rehearsal!" She jumped to her feet. "We haven't used the cameras yet."

"So you're going to kiss him again?"

Silence.

"Cam, you have to believe me," Claire pleaded. "There's nothing going on between me and Conner."

"Correction," he replied. "There's nothing going on between me and *you*."

Click.

Two rotund girls from the catering department burst into hysterics when they passed Massie and Alicia in the studio.

"Your burgers taste like monkey balls!" Alicia hollered, then lowered her voice to a whisper. "Why is everyone laughing at us? First Gina, then the lighting dudes, now the food chicks."

"They probably heard Claire kicked us off the set," Massie murmured. "And they think we're losers."

"But we're on our way to Conner's trailer. How does that make *us* losers?"

"This is all *her* fault," Massie sneered. "Claire Lyons is so D2M." She ditched her sugar-free hot chocolate on a table full of scripts to avoid staining the chocolate-brown cashmere beater she'd bought at Fred Segal. It had been the last one, and she desperately wanted Conner to see her in it while it was still clean. "Fifty gossip points if you can guess why Conner wants to see us."

Alicia tucked her Citizens into her hunter green riding boots for the hundredth time. She'd mistakenly worn the wide pair, and they kept bunching over the tops. "I think he wants to congratulate us. You know, on our final *Daily Grind* show. Maybe he has gifts for us." She hurried to catch up with Massie. "I heard he gave portable DVD players and a copy of all his movies to everyone on his last film."

"What if he's decided to just take one of us to the wrap party tonight?" Massie tried to sound like this would be a bad thing. But she knew that if Conner did make a choice, he would choose her. And there was nothing bad about that.

Alicia stopped. "But what about Abby?"

Massie turned around. "He can't take her. Their romance is a secret, remember? He *has* to take one of us as part of his cover-up." She slid her hand into the pocket of her camouflage capri pants and clutched her lucky cell phone.

"Well, if he asks me, I'll tell him I'm not going without you." Alicia finger-combed her dark, wavy hair.

"Cool." Massie was standing in front of his trailer.

Alicia stomped her foot. "What about *me*? Will you tell him you won't go without *me*?"

"Shhhh." Massie brought her finger to her lips. "His door is open."

"Promise you won't go without me," Alicia whispered.

"Can we puh-lease talk about this later? What if he hears us?" Massie hissed.

"I swear, Lenny," Conner shouted into his cell phone. "I am going to shoot a pumpkin ball up your butt if you don't fix this!"

Massie and Alicia burst out laughing.

"*What* is a pumpkin ball?" Massie giggled into her palm.

Alicia's face was Revlon red. She lifted her hand away from her mouth to say something but cracked up and had to cover it again.

"C'mere." Massie yanked her to the side of the trailer so they could eavesdrop.

"I don't care how you fix it!" Conner roared. "But there's no way she'll go with me *now*."

Massie's underarms itched. Was he talking about *her*?

Conner's voice filled with regret. "I hired you to make her jealous, not to make me look like a loser for hanging out with a booger-leaker and a butt-picker."

Massie and Alicia burst out laughing again and buried their faces in each other's shoulders.

"Don't tell Conner to calm down! Conner has every right to be angry!" He threw a crumpled copy of *US Weekly* at the door.

"Sou-venir!" Alicia whispered as she bent down to pick it up. "Look, his name is in the subscription window. This is totally worth something."

"Lemme see." Massie tore it from her hands.

"Give it back!" Alicia reached for the magazine, but Massie was too quick for her.

"Help me look for coffee stains." She flipped through the celebrity-filled pages. "They might increase the value."

"Give it!" Alicia grabbed for the pages. "I found it."

Massie turned away and kept flipping. "Eh. Ma. Gawd."

"What? Give it!"

"Trust me, you don't want it."

"Yes I do." Alicia ripped it away from Massie.

Her brown eyes widened. "Eh. Ma. Gawd." She leaned against the side of the trailer and slid to the floor.

"Did you read the headline?" She tugged on Massie's

pant leg. "It says, 'Slim Pickings for Conner Foley.' And there's a picture of *us* at his pool!"

"I saw it." Massie sat next to her. She pulled her lucky Motorola out of her pocket and stomped on it with the platform heel of her Frye mules. Purple rhinestones bounced across the studio floor, and plastic phone parts scattered everywhere. "I knew I heard something in the bushes."

Massie had no idea what to do next. No one had ever made a fool of her before.

"I have a booger hanging out of my nose!"

"Well, I'm pulling my bathing suit out of my butt!"

"Now we know why everyone was laughing at us." Alicia brought her knees to her chest and lowered her head. "The whole country reads *US Weekly*," she mumbled. "This is a national disaster."

Massie wanted to grab Alicia by the shoulders, tell her the new revenge plan, and spring into action. She wanted to assure her that these stupid LBRs in Hollywood were no match for them. And remind her that no matter what the stupid magazine said, everyone would still side with the Pretty Committee. But she couldn't. Not this time.

"I don't care if you *tried*, Lenny!" Conner was still furious. "The idea was to make Abby jealous, not to make her dump me for hanging out with . . . Forget your excuses. You're fired!"

Something whacked against the inside wall of his trailer.

"It's a bad day for cell phones." Alicia sighed.

"It's a bad day for everything." Massie pulled her up. "We better get out of here."

"Where are we going to go?"

"Canada."

CURRENT (PATHETIC) STATE OF THE UNION

IN	OUT
Pity party	Wrap party
Press leaks	Booger leaks
Lawsuits	Bathing suits

Rupert was standing by the DJ booth in L.A.'s hottest new club. He had a glass of champagne in one hand and a microphone in the other. "And last but noht least, I'd like to thank my stahs, Connah Foley, Abby Boyd, and Cleh Lyons." He paused for a round of roaring applause.

"That's you, honey." Judi's eyes welled up. "I'm sorry." She dabbed them with the sleeve of her ivory blouse. "I'm just so proud of you."

"Thanks, Mom." Claire grinned.

The applause died and Rupert continued. "Cleh, the moment I saw you I said, 'Emma, I just found the most dahh-ling little loser.'" Everyone laughed. "But seriously." He chuckled. "You have a great deal of talent and the beauty to match. I expect big things from you." He raised his glass. "Cheers."

Claire thanked Rupert with a gracious nod. He blew her an air kiss and she blew one back.

"So you really had *no* experience?" asked Vic Whitestone, the ancient CEO of Gelding Studios.

"Do you count *The Wizard of Oz* at an Orlando junior high school?" she asked.

A group of suit-wearing executives erupted with laughter.

"Well, word is you were simply wonderful," gushed Lauren DiVine, one of the film's producers. "And that you have next-big-thing potential."

"Thank you so much." Claire beamed. "I had a great time."

"Do you see acting as part of your future?" asked Ric Bolster from the Artist Farm, one of the biggest talent agencies in the country.

"Totally." Claire lifted her hand to tug on her bangs but quickly lowered it, remembering that Ahnna had styled them to perfection. "I've always dreamed of acting."

"Well, with your charm, you should have no problem." Ric grinned as he swished the cubes of ice around in his lime-garnished glass.

"I love your outfit." Hannah, the extras coordinator, lifted a mini egg roll off a passing waiter's tray. "The black lace minidress combined with the striped Keds is so fashion-forward. What a cool touch."

"Thanks. Ahnna borrowed the dress from Proenza Schouler and the shoes are mine."

"Divine!"

Claire's face hurt from fake-smiling. She was sure her cheeks would crack into a million pieces if one more person congratulated her on herself. Not that a night of endless compliments from Hollywood's elite was a bad thing. But for some reason, she felt lonely. Like she was filled with holes and the compliments she had been getting were leaking out.

"To Claire, the new girl in town!" shouted Stella, her now-tipsy assistant.

"To Claire!" everyone toasted and cheered.

Their applause started to sound like sizzling bacon as Claire's insides felt carbonated. Her brain no longer seemed attached to her body. Instead, it hovered above a stranger in a designer dress who had just been praised by a famous director.

"I wish your father was here to see all of this." Her mother's eyes glistened.

"I wish a lot of people were here to see all this," Claire mumbled.

Judi threw her arms around her daughter and Claire inhaled the familiar powdery smell of her skin.

"I'm gonna go find Abby." She pulled away before she could start crying. "I'll be right back."

"Okay." Judi wiped her eyes.

Abby was in the center of the dance floor tying a red chiffon scarf around the neck of Conner's stand-in. Everyone formed a circle around them and cheered as she pulled him closer. Conner was the only one who seemed oblivious to her—which was hard to believe, since he was two feet away, grinding Gina's backside.

Looks like dance wars are the new press wars, Claire said to herself, wishing Massie were there to appreciate her observation.

Everyone cleared the floor when the DJ played a Kevin Federline song.

"Abby!" Claire waved.

"Hey." Abby wiped her forehead on some guy's button-down without him noticing.

Claire burst out laughing. Everything was going to be okay. So what if the Pretty Committee hated her? She had new friends now. And they were just as funny.

"How long will you be in Australia?" Claire asked Abby. She missed her already.

"Two months." She popped a finger off a chocolate statue. "It's a first-time director and he isn't as fast as Rupert."

"Maybe I can visit you," Claire offered. "I have some money now."

"Maybe."

"Well, you have to send me your address."

"Why?"

"So I can send you stories about how pathetic everyone is in Westchester."

"Claire, why would you send me stories?"

She stared at Abby blankly. "But wouldn't you want—"

Abby scanned the room, like she was looking for someone. "We were MBFs, not RBFs. I thought you knew that."

"Huh?"

Abby snapped once. "We were *movie* best friends, not *real* best friends."

The carbonation was coming back. "But I thought—"

"I'm starting a new movie and that means new hair, a new crush, and a new BFF." She gripped Claire's shoulders.

"Don't worry." She kissed her on the cheek. "You can totally keep the ring."

Abby raced back to the dance floor, waving her chiffon scarf in the air.

Once again, Claire Lyons stood alone, wondering what she could have possibly done wrong. Another hole formed in her heart. This time everything leaked out.

The DJ suddenly jacked up the music and the entire club became one massive, quaking dance floor. Claire pushed through hordes of sweating, jumping, grinding, whoo-whooing crew members in search of her mother. Luckily, everyone was having too much fun to notice her tears or hear her whimpering as she passed.

"Sweetie, what's wrong?" Judi moved in for another hug but Claire backed away. Contact with a family member would reduce her to a sobbing mess.

"I think I ate some bad shrimp. Can we please go?"

"Of course."

They rushed outside without saying goodbye to anyone and rode back to the hotel in silence. Claire let the hot tears pour out of her while Judi rubbed her head. What did she have to look forward to? Seeing Cam with another girl? Getting kicked out of the Pretty Committee? Stumbling across pictures of Abby and her latest MBF in a magazine? She cried harder. If friends were houses, she'd have been homeless.

The hotel was filled with movie-star look-alikes begging for tables at the Glass Slipper or waiting for the valet to return with their cars. Bursts of laughter exploded like grenades as Claire raced to the elevators, doubting that she'd ever smile again.

"I left the key in the room," Judi called after her. "We have to stop at the front desk and then we can go upstairs and talk about—"

Claire waved, letting her mother know to go without her. How could she possibly tell that sweet woman her daughter was a hopeless loser? It would break her heart.

The elevator was packed with people coming up from the restaurant, but they got out in the lobby. Claire quickly hit twenty-five. And when the doors closed, she burst into stomach-wrenching sobs. If felt good to finally let it all out.

"What's wrong?" Massie asked. "Are you mad we're on *your* elevator?"

Claire whipped her head around. Massie and Alicia were behind her, holding Styrofoam boxes of leftovers, which would inevitably end up in Bean's bowl.

"Maybe you could have your assistant kick us off," Alicia sneered.

Claire quickly dried her eyes and lifted her chin.

"You're home early." Massie sounded delighted. "Something happen?"

Claire sobbed harder. They stared at her with no emotion whatsoever until she was calm enough to speak.

"At least New Yorkers let you know when they don't like you. Here, everyone *acts* like a friend but they're just using you."

"I hear ya." Massie actually sounded sympathetic. "Like when you had us kicked off the set? I *knew* you didn't like us."

"Point." Alicia raised her finger.

"Exactly." Claire felt her cheeks burn. "Like when you planted mustache bleach and athlete's foot cream in my trash, then showed it on TV? I *knew* you didn't like me."

"And when you didn't call me back about dinner?" Massie sneered. "I *knew* you didn't like me."

Claire had pushed that night out of her head. How could she ever have believed Conner and Abby would be her BFFs?

"And when you were too busy laughing with Abby to give us an interview? I *knew* you didn't like *me*." Alicia joined in.

The mention of Abby made Claire's stomach lurch.

"And when you sent Cam a picture of me making out with Conner?"

Ding.

The elevator stopped and the doors opened. Massie and Alicia pushed past her and stormed down the hall. For some reason, the sight of Alicia in her strappy high heels, struggling to keep up with Massie, made Claire giggle. Then her giggle turned into a laugh and her laugh became full-blown hysteria. Her entire face was leaking snot and tears, but none of that mattered. In fact, nothing mattered. And with nothing left, there was nothing to lose. She was finally free.

Massie turned around. "What's so funny?"

Claire, still laughing, grabbed a handful of blue foil-wrapped chocolates off the maid's cart and whipped them at the girls.

"Ouch!" Alicia held her hand in front of her face. "Stop!"

"Kuh-laire, what are you *doing*?"

She grabbed another handful of chocolates and whipped them down the hall.

"Stop it!" Massie snapped.

"Seriously." Alicia held her oversized Fendi in front of her face. "Or you'll regret it."

"What are you going to do?" Claire grabbed more chocolates. "Ignore me? Call me a loser? Make fun of my clothes? Embarrass me on TV? Turn my boyfriend against me?"

The girls were silent.

"Besides . . ." She unleashed another handful of chocolates. "When everyone sees those pictures, you'll be begging for my friendship."

"Point." Alicia glanced at Massie.

"Point," Massie said. Then she bent down, picked up a chocolate, and pelted it at Claire.

It was a direct hit to her eyebrow.

"Ouch!" Claire grabbed her forehead.

As the lump above her left eyebrow got bigger, the holes in Claire's heart got smaller. And suddenly, everything stopped leaking.

```
┌─────────────────────────────────────────┐
│                                         │
│          LE BACCARAT HOTEL              │
│             SUITE 2544                  │
│          Saturday, April 4th            │
│             12:11 A.M.                  │
│                                         │
└─────────────────────────────────────────┘
```

"Who wants these black Joie cargos?" Claire waved the cropped pants over her head like a lasso.

"I already have 'em in white." Alicia shuffled into the bathroom wearing her Le Baccarat slippers and bathrobe. She turned on the sink and started brushing her teeth with an electric toothbrush.

"I have 'em in olive." Massie did up the buttons on her father's old Brooks Brothers shirt-turned-pajama-top. It was her secret way of staying close to him while she was away. "Put them in K's pile."

Claire whipped them on top of a pile marked KRISTEN: FEMININE-SPORTY.

The girls had gone through all seven comps boxes, dividing the clothes as they saw fit.

Claire's "Casual-Comfy" Pile
Designers Include:
C&C   Juicy Couture
Velvet   Splendid

Massie's "Trendy-Chic" Pile
Designers Include:

Ella Moss	DKNY
BCBG	Lauren Moffatt

Alicia's "Flirty-Classic" Pile*
Designers Include:

Theory	Ya-Ya
Marc Jacobs	Charlotte Ronson

*(*Ralph Lauren withdrew his comps because Claire refused to wear him exclusively while in Los Angeles. It hurt Alicia more than it hurt Ralph.)*

Kristen's "Feminine-Sporty" Pile
Designers Include:

Chip & Pepper	Diesel
Joie	Vince

Dylan's "Loud and Proud" Pile
Designers Include:

L.A.M.B.	Betsey Johnson
Miss Sixty	Alice + Olivia

Layne's "Reject" Pile
Includes:
A handbag shaped like a cell phone
Polka-dot espadrilles
A belt made of gum wrappers
A J.Lo by Jennifer Lopez T-shirt

"How are we going to pack all of this?" Massie collapsed on her pile.

"Stella said she'd have it shipped home for us," Claire replied.

"I just stopped hating her," Massie murmured into her turquoise-and-brown tank top.

Ding.

"Is that my computer?" Alicia called from the bathroom.

"Yup." Claire jumped to her feet. "Want me to check it?"

"It's not Cam." Massie rolled her eyes.

"How do you know?" she asked.

"Because it's . . ." She checked her Coach watch. "Three fifteen in the morning back home. Besides, why would he be e-mailing you on Alicia's computer?"

Claire tugged the navy blue string on her new Juicy sweats. "I e-mailed him while you guys were going through the fourth comp box."

Massie was about to lecture Claire on the art of playing it cool but held her tongue. After all, it was her fault they were fighting. The least she could do was be supportive. "What did you write?"

"I'm not telling." Claire blushed.

"I'll just go look in her sent mail." Massie pushed herself off the floor and raced into the living room.

"Noooo!" Claire giggle-screamed. "Don't you dare!" She charged after her.

Massie stopped in front of the computer. "False alarm."

"Who is it?" Alicia rubbed a cotton ball across her oil-free T-zone.

"It's Dylan and Kristen." Massie felt sick of saying their names. She had been leaving them messages all week and neither one of them had bothered returning her calls. She had overcome the humiliation of losing the movie to Claire but if one of them stole Derrington, she would—

Alicia clicked accept.

"Hey!" Dylan and Kristen waved. They were sitting on Massie's bed, each wearing a pair of her satin Victoria's Secret pj's.

"I gave you permission to sleep at my house, not raid my closet," Massie snapped. "And why aren't you sleeping?"

"I told you she'd be mad," Dylan said to Kristen.

Massie knew her greeting was harsh. But what did they expect?

"Well, you won't be mad when you hear *this*." Kristen beamed. "We were going to wait and tell you in person but we couldn't sleep without telling you—"

"Lemme guess. You and Derrington lip-kissed in the middle of the soccer field?"

"What?" Kristen gasped.

"I know why you've been avoiding me."

"You do?" Kristen crinkled her forehead.

"Yeah, it's because you've been hanging out with Derrington." Massie's voice shook. She'd had no idea how upset she was until she heard herself say the words.

"*And* Josh," Alicia added.

Dylan reached into a cereal box. "I guess *that's* why they're going to be at your welcome-home party tomorrow."

"*Dylan!*" Kristen smacked her so hard she choked on her bran flakes.

"A surprise party?" Alicia squealed.

"Yeah." Kristen shoved Dylan.

"Sorry." Dylan chewed. "Don't tell anyone I told you."

"Is Derrington going?" Massie asked.

"Of course," Kristen said.

"Yay!" Massie shouted, letting her excitement show. Why not? If he dumped her, she could handle it. If this trip had taught her one thing, it was that she could survive rejection and humiliation—maybe even triumph from them.

"What about Josh?"

"Yup," Dylan said between chews.

"Is Cam going to be there?" Claire asked.

"Uh . . ." Dylan looked to Kristen for backup.

"Uh . . ." She cleared her throat. "He didn't mention anything. But that doesn't mean—"

"Massie!" Claire stomped her foot.

"Okay, okay. It will all be fixed in the morning. Pinky-swear."

Claire locked pinkies with Massie and shook.

"Then why haven't you called us back?" Alicia asked. "Is everyone laughing at us? Are you embarrassed to be friends with a butt-picker and a booger-leaker?"

Massie's stomach lurched. It was the one thing she had been afraid to ask. "Are we so done?"

"Done?" Dylan slapped another handful of bran flakes in her mouth. "Done? Ehmagawd, no! You're the opposite of done. You're un-done!"

"Everyone wants you to sign their magazines." Kristen shook her copy of *US Weekly*. She flipped to page seventeen. "You are swimming at Conner Foley's house. *Conner Foley!*" She fell back on the bed and shook her legs in the air.

"But what about my booger?"

"And my wedgie?"

"You were at Conner Foley's house!" Kristen shouted.

"Point." Alicia lifted her finger.

A tingle shot up Massie's spine. "Now that I think about it, this is the best thing that could have happened to us."

"How?" Alicia had an I'm-so-not-buying-it look on her face.

"We always knew pictures of us with celebs would put the Pretty Committee back on top. And these are way better than Claire's amateur shots—"

"Thanks!" Claire smirked.

"Ehmagawd!" Massie slapped her hand over her mouth. "I didn't mean it like that. It's just that these were professionally taken and printed in *US Weekly*. It's like our plan times ten."

"It's okay." Claire smiled. "I know what you meant. This *is* better."

"Ehmagawd! And wait! I have something *even* better." Massie hurried to the walk-in closet and grabbed her metallic Juicy Couture tote. When she was directly in front of the iSight camera and in full view of everyone, she pulled out Conner's CF jeans. "Ta-da!"

"No way!" Alicia slapped her thigh. "I forgot you had those."

"What are they?" Kristen asked.

Massie turned the jeans around and held the unmistakable back pocket up to the computer.

"Ahhhhh!" Dylan, Kristen, and Claire shouted.

"I found them in Conner's cuh-ban-ya," Alicia bragged. "I got one thousand goss—"

"And I stole them," Massie chimed in, before Alicia could take all the credit. She was waving the jeans in the air like a victory flag when something fell on her head.

Everyone burst into hysterics.

Massie grabbed the object and held it in front of her face. "Ew! It's his Hugo Boss underwear!" She threw them at Alicia, who tossed them at Claire.

"What is with all the random underwear on this trip?" Claire burst out laughing.

"Huh?" Massie said.

"First there was the pair of Harry Potter briefs I found in my brother's hockey bag. Then there was the pair Abby threw at the—"

"Wait!" A familiar prickle of heat spread across Massie's palms. She was on the verge of a devious scheme. "What does that clock say?"

"Twelve thirty-five," Claire answered.

Massie shook her head, then half-smiled at Alicia, hoping she'd catch on. "What does that clock say?" She tried again.

"Twelve thirty-five in the morning?"

"No."

"Ehmagawd!" Alicia flapped her hands. "Payback time!"

"Yup." Massie smiled. "Claire, get the Harry Potters. Kristen, Google the photographer who took those photos. I think his name was Lenny. I need a phone number or an address. Alicia, get me the concierge desk."

"What can I do?" Dylan begged through a mouthful of cereal.

"You can stop eating bran. It's making me sick."

"Thank gawd." She threw the box on the floor of Massie's bedroom.

Massie giggled. It felt good to be in control again.

"I have the concierge." Alicia covered the phone with her hand. "What should I tell him?"

"We have a package that needs to be picked up and held for a guy named Lenny. He'll be by to get it in the morning."

"Done." Alicia relayed the message.

"Got it!" Kristen announced. "His last name is Richards. Leonard Richards. He works at *US Weekly*."

"Get me his voice mail," Massie insisted.

"I did already." Kristen beamed.

Massie put her Razr on speakerphone and dialed Leonard's number. While it rang, Claire gave Massie Todd's underwear.

After five rings, the photographer's voice mail picked up. Massie took a deep breath and lifted the phone to her mouth.

"Hey, Lenny, it's Abby Boyd," she snapped into the phone. Claire gasped.

"Shhhh." Alicia covered Claire's mouth.

Massie continued, "My *ex*-boyfriend Conner Foley left his jeans and Harry Potter underwear in my hotel room. They'll be at the front desk of the Le Baccarat Hotel, waiting for you. He dumped me for that ah-dorable reporter on *The Daily Grind*. Her name is Massie Block—that's M-A-S-S-I-E B-L-O-C-K. And FYI, she won't give him the time of day."

She snapped her phone shut and everyone cracked up.

"We better get some beauty sleep." Alicia yawned, then lowered her voice to a whisper. "For our party."

"And we have to pick outfits and—"

"Wait!" Kristen interrupted Massie. "Don't you want to know why we never called you back last week?"

"Oh yeah." Massie wondered how she could have possibly forgotten such a major detail. "Why didn't you?"

"We were writing an essay on the meaning of life." Dylan sounded very pleased with herself. "We even pulled an all-nighter."

"*You* wrote a paper?" Massie folded her arms across her chest.

"Well, Kristen did," Dylan admitted. "But I made the Xeroxes and put them in cute folders."

"Zzzzzzz." Massie fake-snored, hoping they would get to the point already.

"The OCD board meeting was tonight." Kristen sounded irritated.

"Ehmagawd!" Massie's throat locked. Why hadn't her mother mentioned it?

"Last week I asked if I could go," Kristen continued. "I thought if Principal Burns saw me crying about my scholarship, she'd feel bad and let me back in. But no students were allowed. So I wrote the paper and gave it to your dad and Mr. Rivera to read."

"The paper was soooo good," Dylan gushed. "I couldn't understand *any* of it."

"What was it about?" Claire asked.

"It's called 'The Meaning of Life Is Get a Life,'" Kristen said.

"And?"

"Well . . ." Her lips curled. "It's my philosophy on why we should be given a second chance."

"We?" Massie felt a tinge of hope.

"Given." Dylan beamed. "Kristen signed all of our names, so they think we wrote it together."

"Even mine?" Claire asked.

"Are you still living in Massie's guesthouse?" Dylan teased.

Claire nodded.

"Then yes, even you."

"And?" Massie was suddenly interested.

"*And it worked! We're back!*" Kristen shouted.

Everyone screamed. Bean ran and hid under the bed.

"On one condition," Kristen added.

The girls became silent.

"We have to get more of a 'life.'" She made air quotes.

"Huh?" Massie asked. "What does *that* mean?"

"It *means* we have to sign up for extracurricular activities.

Since I'm on the soccer team I'm covered, but you guys each have to sign up for a sport. "

"But I can't run," Alicia whined. "Did you mention that?"

"Then join a club," Dylan suggested. "That's probably what I'll do."

"Ew, why?" Alicia winced.

"Principal Burns doesn't want us shopping after school anymore. She thinks it's a shallow waste of time and money and would like us to do something more meaningful."

"Yes!" Claire exclaimed.

"This is in-sane!" Massie shouted. "Where did she get such a *stupid* idea?"

"From Kristen's paper." Dylan rolled her eyes. "That's the only part I understood."

"Ehmagawd, I'm dead." Alicia buried her head in her hands.

Kristen grinned. "Can you believe it worked? I got us in!"

"Thanks." Massie smiled, knowing the minute she got home she would have to dedicate her life to finding a way out of this. She had suffered enough humiliation for one year. And she was determined to finish the seventh grade in style . . . not sneakers.

Claire closed her photo album and leaned against the black leather seat of the Range Rover. She'd spent most of the six-hour flight from Los Angeles studying the pictures given to her by the cast and crew of *Dial L for Loser*. There were shots of everything—her on the set, getting direction from Rupert, Stella feeding her Red Vines, the baseball game they'd played with the extras, and her and Emma driving a golf cart. Even the ones of Abby made her smile. Standing shoulder-to-shoulder in their matching uniforms pretending to be Siamese twins, Conner trying to give them piggybacks at the same time, and a close-up of Abby's rings.

"You okay?" Massie nudged her arm.

Claire opened her eyes and smiled. "Yeah."

"Is it Cam?"

She nodded and wiped the tear off her cheek. She wasn't about to tell Massie how much she missed her "movie family" or how much she'd loved acting and living in sunny California. Why make her jealous all over again?

"I told you I'd fix things with him." Massie placed her hand on Claire's armrest.

"I know. Thanks."

"Can we get back to our game?" Alicia whispered. "We're almost home."

"Okay," Massie whispered back. "My turn." She leaned toward the front seat and tapped the side of her mother's arm. "So, uh, what's with all the cars on our street?"

Alicia gave her two thumbs-up.

"Uh, one of the neighbors must be having a party." Kendra twirled the diamond stud in her ear.

Claire turned to the window to keep from laughing. During their drive from the airport, the girls had taken turns trying to get Isaac and the mothers to crack and accidentally spill the details of the surprise party. The winner was to get five hundred gossip points. But as Isaac turned into the circular driveway of the Blocks' estate, it became clear that unless they tried harder, this game would not have a winner.

"Wait, Isaac, aren't you taking me home?" Alicia asked when he turned off the engine.

Claire and Massie kicked each other in the backseat. Alicia winked.

"Oh, I totally forgot." He hit his head against the steering wheel, then looked at the moms for backup.

"Uh, that's my fault." Judi tried to turn around, but she was sandwiched between Isaac and Kendra and couldn't move. "I needed to get home and let the exterminator in, so I asked Isaac to drop me first."

"Exterminator?" Claire sounded squeamish. "Ew! I'm staying in a hotel!"

Kendra chuckled.

258

"It's nothing to worry about," Judi assured her.

"Hey, since you're here, Alicia, why don't you stay for lunch? Isaac can take you home after you eat," Kendra offered.

"Thanks anyway, but I should go."

The girls doubled over and laughed silently into their hands.

"I insist." Kendra opened her door.

"Um, okay." Alicia shrugged, as though she had given up.

Claire heard the familiar crunching of gravel under her Keds when she stepped out of the Range Rover. The trees in front of the house were still bare, the sky was its usual milky gray, and William Block's black Mercedes was gleaming. Even the air smelled the same; like fresh-cut grass and cold water. But something about home looked completely different than it had three weeks ago. Or maybe it was the way Claire was seeing it.

The tennis courts, the pools, the luxury cars, the designer clothes, the expensive jewelry and enormous leather handbags that used to make her feel inadequate no longer had an effect on her. She finally saw them for what they were. Like the hallway set of Lakeview Middle School, these things were used to create an illusion. But behind their shiny exteriors lay a tangle of wires and cables and confusion. And no one, not even the Pretty Committee, had found a way to sort it all out.

"Rate me." Massie finger-combed her extensions as she teetered on the gravel in her BCBG wedges. She was wearing a red Lauren Moffatt dress (from the comp box) over a pair of skinny Sass & Bide jeans.

"Nine-point-two." Alicia twisted the cap on her MAC Lipglass. "Me?"

Massie scanned Alicia, from the top of her silky black hair, past her gray Theory Maddox jacket (comp box), white True Religion jeans, and black ballet flats. Then back up again. "Nine."

They looked at Claire, who was wearing the same green doctor's scrubs, faded long-sleeved tee, and black-and-white Keds she'd worn on the way to L.A. The only new thing she wore was the yellow pinky ring Abby had given her. "Don't bother," she said with a knowing smile.

"Fall back," Massie said.

Claire and Alicia stopped walking and let the mothers pull ahead.

"What's our plan?" she whispered once her mother unlocked the front door to the main house.

"What do you mean?" Claire asked.

"I mean, as we speak, there are at least a hundred people in my living room waiting to surprise us. We have to act shocked."

"Kuh-laire, any acting tips?" Alicia raised her dark eyebrows.

"Can we please stop with the—"

"I'm serious!" she insisted.

"Yeah, give us a tip."

Claire studied their faces looking for sneers, lip twitches, or wandering eyes. But she saw nothing but pure sincerity.

"Okay." She rolled her shoulders and thought of the advice Rupert gave her on the first day of shooting. "Focus on your breathing. And clear your mind of everything. Be in the moment. Don't walk in the house thinking about the people who are waiting for you or how you'll react when you see them. Just walk in thinking about the step you are taking at that exact second. That way, when they yell surprise, you'll be surprised."

"Hmmmm." Massie nodded slowly, like she was sizing up DKNY's new spring line. "I like it."

"Okay then, start breathing." Claire inhaled deeply and began walking toward the house. But every crunching step brought her closer to the moment of truth. Closer to getting an answer to the one question she'd asked herself over and over again on the six-hour flight back from Los Angeles. And she wasn't sure she was ready for it.

"Massie!" Kendra poked her head out of the door like she was someone paying for a pizza in a bathrobe. "Would you mind running to the spa and getting me a bottle of Evian? The fridge is empty and I can't find Inez."

Alicia and Claire giggled.

"Sure, no problem," Massie replied without hesitation.

"Why aren't you fighting her on it?" Alicia asked. "Don't you want the gossip points?"

"She ahb-viously needs time to hide everyone. Anyway, we can check our hair and stuff while we're in there. It's perfect."

"Point," Alicia said as they stepped onto the cold, stiff grass and began making their way across the lawn to the old horse shed.

"It feels kind of good to be back." Massie looked around the sprawling estate.

"Ah-greed."

"Don't you miss the warm weather?" Claire folded her arms across her chest. "Or the hotel? Or the people we met?"

They exchanged glances, then shook their heads.

"Do you?" Massie asked.

Claire shrugged, then tried to refocus on her breathing.

"Are you going to lip-kiss Derrington when you see him?" Alicia asked.

"I dunno. Maybe." She giggled, then opened the door. "I kind of hope so—"

"SURPRISE!"

"Ehmagawd!" shouted Massie and Alicia at the exact same time.

Claire was too stunned to call Apple-C.

The spa was decorated with colorful "Welcome Home" banners and handmade *Dial L for Loser* movie posters that had been cut from the same poster board Layne used to make her protest signs. Tables filled with cakes and cookies and sandwiches and sushi were in every corner of the room. And every person whom Claire had ever met since she'd moved to Westchester was there. Well, almost everyone.

Jay Lyons was the first to greet her with a giant hug. "I am so proud of you," he whispered in her ear.

"Thanks, Dad." Claire felt a lump in her throat. "I missed you."

"I missed you too, Claire Bear. Enjoy the party. You deserve it." He hugged her one last time, then headed straight for the waiter with the tray of chicken fingers.

Claire reached into the pocket of her scrubs and pulled the last gummy worm out of the shredded plastic bag. With a quick cough, she stuffed it in her mouth and held it on her tongue. It tasted like loneliness.

"Thank gawd you're back!" Dylan and Kristen threw their arms around the girls, practically knocking them onto giant cutouts of Massie and Alicia taken from *US Weekly*. Stacks of the magazine were piled on a nearby table, waiting to be autographed.

The flat-screen TV usually reserved for Kendra's yoga DVDs played the *Daily Grind* segments on a constant loop. And the paparazzi shots of Claire, Conner, and Abby hung from the ceiling rafters like giant mobiles.

"Where's the movie star?" Layne shouted. She was wearing a brown pantsuit with a pink Hello Kitty tee underneath.

"Hey!" Claire broke away from the Pretty Committee and gave her friend a hug. "Layne, have you seen—"

"We got you!" Judi interrupted as she entered the spa holding a massive red cake in the shape of an *L*.

"You did!" Claire was about to thank her mother for helping to plan such a great party when she was pulled away by the ex–Country Club girls, who wanted to know every last detail about Conner Foley.

"He's a really nice guy. A lot of fun to work with," Claire heard herself say as she continued searching the room for Cam.

Derrington and Josh were by the treadmills, increasing the speed and incline, trying to see who could hold on longer. Two bouquets of daisies were on the floor by their jackets, waiting as the boys worked up the nerve to deliver them.

"Is it so weird being back here?" asked Strawberry, the former leader of Da Crew and the only girl at OCD with enough nerve to dye her hair pink. "You know, now that you're friends with all these famous people, we must seem so lame to you."

"I don't think you're lame." She forced a kind smile.

"Thanks," Strawberry gushed. "So, are you rich now?"

"Uh . . ." Claire remembered her parents telling her not to tell anyone how much money she made because it was tacky. "I can definitely buy a few new things for spring, you know, if I want to."

"Awesome." Strawberry stared at her with giddy fascination.

"Hey, loser." Todd tapped Claire on the shoulder. He was wearing a T-shirt that said MY SISTER IS MORE FAMOUS THAN YOUR SISTER. His little friend Tiny Nathan was standing beside him nibbling on a mozzarella stick.

"Hey!" Claire turned her back to Strawberry and bent to hug her brother.

"Easy!" He pushed her away. "Calm yourself, woman."

"Relax." Claire rolled her eyes. "I was trying to get away from that stalker. It had nothing to do with you." She mussed her brother's red hair. "But it is good to—"

"Yeah, yeah." Todd kicked Tiny Nathan in the shin.

"Ow!" He grabbed his leg. "Whadd'ya do that for?"

Todd shrugged. "Sorry."

"Here." Todd reached into the pocket of his Levi's. "This is for you." He pulled out a bag of gummy worms and slapped them into Claire's palm.

Her heart felt heavy with sadness. "Thanks." She tried to smile. But it was impossible for her to look at a gummy without seeing Cam.

"Wait, there's more." Todd reached inside his pocket. This time he pulled out a crumpled piece of paper. He tossed it at Claire, then chased Tiny Nathan into the "wet section" of the spa.

Claire caught it and squeezed it in her fist, unsure of what to do next. What if it was from Cam? Or worse, what if it wasn't? But wait, who else would it be from? She made a break for the door and managed to slip out undetected.

The cold air did nothing for her sweaty pits and clammy hands, but it still felt good. Once she was sure no one was around, Claire sat on the frozen grass and unfolded the note slowly, as if it were an explosive that could detonate in her face.

She inhaled courage, exhaled fear, then read.

C,
Meet me behind out back.
C

She read the C-note three more times, then stuffed it in the pocket of her scrubs.

"Cam?" She stood. "Are you out here?"

"Hey." He rounded the side of the shed.

Claire stared at the boy who'd filled her thoughts for the last three weeks, wondering where to begin. A hug? An apology? A neck-sniff?

"Did you get my e-mail last night?"

He looked at her with his blue eye and green eye and nodded.

"Well?"

He put his hands in the pockets of his leather jacket. "I'm here, aren't I?"

"Yes, you are." Claire started to smile.

"Yes, I am." He smiled back.

"So you forgive me?"

"Massie called me three times to explain." He took a step toward her. "So yes, I forgive you."

Her stomach fluttered.

"So are you really going to show me what you learned on set? Or were you kidding when you wrote that?"

"I wasn't kidding." Claire giggled when she thought of her bold e-mail.

Cam took another step.

Then another.

And another.

Without thinking, Claire hurried toward him and pressed her lips against his. They were cold but soft. She pulled back for a split second, took a breath, and then leaned in again, only this time slower. And on the count of three she poked her tongue into his mouth. He met it with his and—

Cl-eh, Cl-eh.

Cl-eh, Cl-eh.

Claire pulled away from Cam and looked over her shoulder. Her heart was pounding from the kiss and the excitement of seeing him again.

"Is that your phone?" he asked.

"Oh." She felt her cheeks redden. "Yeah. Sorry." She pulled it out of her jacket pocket and answered.

"Hello?"

"Please hold for Miles Baime," crackled a woman's voice on the other end. After a brief pause, she returned. "You're on."

An authoritative man took over. "Claire Lyons, Miles Baime."

"Uh, hi?"

"I'm a talent agent at The Artist Farm." He paused for a reaction, but Claire had no idea what to say.

"I saw some selects from *Dial L for Loser*, and I think you're a real natural. I'd like to represent you and take you to the top."

"Seriously?" Claire shouted.

"What is it?" Cam dug his hands in his pockets.

She lifted her finger as if to say, *I'll tell you in a minute.*

"Dead serious. Can you swing by my office on Monday?"

"Uh, I'm back in Westchester."

"Well then, we'll have work on a plan to move you out here," Miles said over the click-clack of his keyboard.

"Uh, okay." Claire was stunned. "I mean, let me think about it. I mean, let me talk to my parents."

Miles gave her his number and insisted she call him first thing Monday morning.

Claire snapped her phone shut. Did she really have a future as an actress?

"Who was that?" Cam kicked the frozen grass with his black-and-white Adidas.

"Some Hollywood agent guy," Claire said, very slowly. "He wants me to move to California." She blinked. "And become an actress."

"You're not going to do it, are you?" he asked. "You know, now that you're back at OCD?"

Claire rubbed her thumb over the red rhinestones on her phone and imagined her life in California. Sunshine, sand, and palm trees, just like Florida. She would be the center of attention and the girl everyone wanted to hang out with. But the best part would be the acting. She'd get paid to do something she loved.

Then she thought of Massie's Friday night sleepovers and Layne and OCD and her family. . . .

She lifted her eyes and looked at Cam.

"How could you leave all this?" He waved his arm at the Blocks' stone mansion, their pool, and tennis court.

How could I not? she wanted to say. But instead she grabbed his hand and led him back into the party, trying her hardest to follow Rupert's advice and live in that one moment.